MW01714234

Shakespeare's Tales

A Collie's Perspective

Vincent L. Morris
Shakespeare "collie" Morris

To my good friends
Pat and Jeanine.
Enjoy.
Vince

Shakespeare's Tales: A Collie's Perspective Copyright © 2019 by Vincent L. Morris. All Rights Reserved.

All rights reserved. No part of this book may be reproduced in any form or by any electronic or mechanical means including information storage and retrieval systems, without permission in writing from the author. The only exception is by a reviewer, who may quote short excerpts in a review.

Cover designed by Vincent L. Morris with assistance from Kindle Direct Publishing

This book is a work of fiction. Names, characters, places, and incidents either are products of the author's imagination or are used fictitiously. Any resemblance to actual persons, living or dead, events, or locales is entirely coincidental.

Printed in the United States of America

First Printing: 2019
Kindle Direct Publishing

ISBN-13 9781795779807

Dedicated to all animal lovers and their special friends. The last tale, Gray Wolf, is meant as a tribute to the Cree Nation and their deep respect and love for the land and its animal inhabitants. It is in no way meant to detract from or supplant their legends and stories that have so much to teach all of us.

Contents

Preface

This is a book for the whimsical. Do you ever look into an animal's eyes and wonder what it is thinking? Well, it wasn't until I came to know a remarkable individual that I had the chance to find out. No, I didn't meet Dr. Dolittle. There are people who have such a love for animals that they can establish a close bond. My younger daughter Lauren is one of these people. Sometimes riders even claim they can relay their intentions to horses through their body movements and signals, but I am talking about an individual who can actually communicate with other species in their own language. I am referring to a collie named Shakespeare. When Shakespeare came into our household as a puppy, my wife Alice and I had no idea that a genius was entering our lives. He seemed like any other puppy, scampering about, getting into mischief, loving his treats. However, when I went to my computer, he would whine to come up on my lap. He then seemed to watch very intently as my fingers typed out messages. Every once in a while, he would hit one of the keys with his paw. He even typed out a few words on occasion; I dismissed these actions as happenstance and never gave them much thought. Shakespeare did always seem to listen with particular intensity when my wife and I spoke to each other. Not only did he learn verbal commands very quickly, but he actually seemed to understand what we were saying when we were just talking to each other. When he heard the word *food*, he would immediately run to his dish, or if we said *bath*, he would hide. But I discounted this ability as his recognition of only a few words. After all, a lot of dogs can do this.

As a few of you may know, I have great literary ambitions and have even published a book of sonnets called, *Love's Passion, Pleasure Through Poetry.* Alas, while I can write passable poetry, I just can't get the hang of prose. There are a lot of stories in my head, but I can never get them down in a form anyone wants to read. As you'll discover in the first tale in this book, "Shakespeare's Own Tale," my literary fortunes changed for the better when I accidently came across Shakespeare's blog on line, where he had written his own story. I was stunned by his writing skill and immediately decided that he could give my stories the voice and wit they so desperately needed, but I could never provide. After some very tough negotiating, I managed to convince Shakespeare to team up with me. The wisdom of my liaison with Shakespeare was confirmed when I discovered that, in addition to English and his native Dog, Shakespeare was fluent in Cat and Horse. Between us, we could directly provide both human and animal view-points to our stories.

Both Shakespeare and I share a common interest in conveying how much humans and animals can benefit by helping one another; sometimes they can even save each other's lives. Thus, we thoroughly reject the concept of people owning dogs, cats, horses or any pets. Everyone should welcome them into their lives like friends and appreciate how much we do for each other. I hope you enjoy Shakespeare's tales as much as I do. If enough of you express your appreciation tangibly, perhaps this won't be the last of his tales to be told!

Vincent L. Morris

If it wasn't for my fur, my blushing face would be apparent. Even though my intellect is vastly superior to Vince's, he has provided a lot of the raw material for at least some of my stories. I really have become fond of Vince's well-meaning, but inept attempts at relating a story and am happy to share the spotlight with him. I realize that my literary skills attack the iconoclastic views of literary critics who believe that human writings are the only ones worth perusing. Despite the expostulate and supercilious views of these *so-called* pundits, I join Vince in hoping you find my tales entertaining and didactic. At the risk of seeming crass, I am asking you to **please buy this book,** so I can convince Vince to take me on a world cruise with him and Alice. Just think of all the tales I'll be able to relate to you then!
Shakespeare 'collie' Morris

Tale One: Shakespeare's Own Tale

Baby Shakespeare

Even as a puppy, Shakespeare was trying to figure out our quaint English language, so he could fulfill his dream of becoming a great poet and author.

Vince: *I am the human parent of a collie, Shakespeare. My association with Shakespeare has graphically demonstrated to me that, although humans would like to claim the dominant species title for themselves, if you examine the facts honestly, it becomes clear that this idea is simply not tenable.*

Shakespeare: *I obviously am part of the preeminent species because the facts demonstrate themselves very clearly! I only have to yip that I'm hungry or need to go outside to do my business, and Vince comes running. I only need to demand a walk, and Vince is beside me, lead in hand. He always buys me bones to chew and gives me stupendous scratches whenever I enjoin these. I rest my case.*

Vince: *Shakespeare's aspirations to become a writer started when he was a puppy. He has always had the ability, but mastering English and the keyboard on my computer were the main things holding him back. Typing was made even harder by the size of the keys that were small compared to the size of his paws. I know all this because he later confided in me. After watching the keystrokes, as I engaged in my pathetic attempts to write, Shakespeare finally gained the skills to write his own first story – something that only became apparent to me when I came across his website, www.shakespeare.dog, on my computer one day. Thus,* ***Shakespeare's Own Tale begins.***

Shakespeare's Own Tale

They say dogs can't write,
But I have proved them quite wrong.
Please enjoy my tales.

WOW, I NOW HAVE A VOICE. It took me a while to observe and master the English language and computer keyboard skills from Vince, but I have now become adroit at these talents.

My first memory is Mom. She's great. She allows me to snuggle up and get milk. She licks me in all the right places to keep me clean. When I grow up, I have to do all this for myself. My human caregivers – notice I don't say owners – indicate their disgust when I clean my private parts. What do they want me to do? *They* don't go around with a dirty butt! Anyway, my mom and I live in this building with my brothers and sisters and a bunch of other dogs. Mom calls it a kennel. Our human caregivers don't really interact with us too much. Don't get me wrong, they're okay. Once I'm old enough to not suckle milk from Mom, they give me food and fresh water and occasionally pick me up and pet me. When I ask Mom about this arrangement, she says that it is all she has known, and she is always treated well.

As I get older, the humans let me out in a fenced-in pen. It's fun to scramble around and chase my brothers and sisters. One day, I'm playing on the grass with one of my buddies when a male and female human come into the yard. "Blah blah blah blah. Blah, blah blah blah blah blah blah?" she asks. This is before I learn the humans' rather peculiar language. With that, she scoops me up, and my life changes forever. The female holds me as we enter this big box with seats. When it starts to move, my stomach becomes a little queasy, but as she pets me and says with a quiet, loving voice, "Blah, blah, blah blah," I do feel a little better. When we stop, she gets out and takes me through this door into my new domain. It's almost embarrassing how much they lavish upon me. I have my own food dish, which they fill at regular intervals. It's nice not to have to scramble to get a good place at the *old feeding trough*. Now, I do keep knocking over the water pail. It isn't my fault that it has such high sides, and nobody told me I can't put my paw in it! Finally, after several accidents, they get the message and buy a water dish that isn't so easy to tip over.

Communication with my caregivers has been a major problem. It first comes up when I'm trying to house-train my humans. It should be simple, right? I tell them I have to go, and they take me outside. Well, they always seem to be preoccupied with this box with flashing lights and funny sounds. I go right up to them and clearly tell them I must go *now*! But they ignore me and keep on watching their stupid box. I become more persistent, and all I get is angry yells. So, I give up and go into a quiet, unused room to do my business. Then, all of a sudden, everyone seems to notice. They bring out a myriad of things – rags, soap, water pails – and engage in a frantic cleaning regimen. You think they'd immediately get the picture, but it takes several of these incidents before they learn. Now, at my first yip at them, I'm out the door in a flash! Among all their attempts to communicate, a repetitious word pattern –

Shakespeare - begins to emerge. I finally figure out that this sound refers to me, you know, like a name. Anyway, when I respond, it seems to make my caregivers happy, so I humour them. Similarly, my female caregiver calls the male, Vince, and he called the female, Alice. I infer that those are their names. They also have two daughters, they call Laurel and Lauren. I love them and really enjoy playing fetch with them.

Our communication issues don't really improve until Vince and Alice finally admit that they need obedience training. They think the instruction is for me, but we all know who really needs to be schooled! The classroom is a big, open room with rubber mats on the floor, in case our caregivers don't clue in when we dogs have to go out to do our business. First of all, the teachers let everyone get acquainted. After we all have a chance to sniff each other's rear ends, we have fun chasing and scampering around. Then it's time to get down to work. The instructors start by teaching our caregivers some basic commands. I don't mind because there's always food involved, yum! Vince is instructed to say, *sit*, and then holds some food over my head, which naturally causes me to sit. They similarly use food to help our caregivers learn how to get us to lie down, stand, and come – all to their commands.

One command we use every day is *heel*. I don't mind because it means we are doing one of my favorite things, taking a walk. Not only do I get to relieve myself, but I can chase and chew on fallen branches. I do love to chase sticks. It's especially fun when other dogs are around. Then we can play keep-away with our retrieved treasure of a thrown stick. Now we dogs are a lot more ecologically minded than humans. They keep buying these plastic, non-recyclable toys. Some of them are actually dangerous, since they contain plastic pieces, which become sharp shards when we chew on them. I hate to think what would happen if we swallowed one. No, we dogs just prefer good old wooden sticks. They are free.

They are biodegradable. They are easier on the teeth than some of the hard toys humans buy. But, unfortunately, pet stores don't consult with us before buying what humans think we will like.

I should now cover the topic of smells and noses. As far as noses go, I'm not sure why humans even have them. I mean, they can't smell a scent unless it is screaming at them. When we go out, my nose gives me a chance to catch up on the news of the day – which of my dog friends has been by and at what time. Even for strangers, I can tell approximately how many dogs have been there and how long ago. I can also detect other non-canine animals, such as squirrels or rabbits. But, some of my buddies tell me about another animal that should be avoided at all costs. This animal looks a little like a black and white cat, but it engages in chemical warfare when threatened. Yes, you guessed correctly, it's a skunk. Well, one day a poor buddy of mine is just doing what dogs are expected to do – chase and bark at this pseudo cat – when it lifts its tail, and this green cloud hits my friend right between the eyes. My buddy tells me it makes his eyes burn and the stench won't go away no matter how much he rubs his face on the ground. My buddy also relates that after seven baths and goodness knows how many concoctions, he still stinks. It is so bad that even the humans can smell it! When I'm out walking, I noticed that he even has to sleep outside for many sunrises after this event. Now, just the sight of anything black and white has him running the other way!

There's one more point about communication that I should cover – barking. It took a while, but I finally taught Vince and Alice that a high-pitched yip means that I need food and/or to relieve myself. But, as for my full-throated bark, they just don't seem to get it. A perfect stranger can walk by, sometimes cutting right across our property; I don't know if he plans to attack us or what! When I give my repeated, protective barks, Vince and Alice yell at me, "Stop making so much noise." Well, isn't that the point when raising the alarm? And, what about when people go by with carts that have high-pitched squeaky wheels – it hurts my ears – '*shrieky* SQUEEK, *shrieky* SQUEEK'? It just drives me crazy, but I don't see my caregivers yelling at them!

As I mature, I become more and more aware of my body equipment and realize that girl dogs and boy dogs are quite different. It's amazing how much I can find out about any of my canine friends by just smelling a butt. If it's a female, you instinctively know how mature she is; how receptive she is to your advances. For males, there is a whole dominance thing. When we go to the park, I notice that dogs hump each other. Now humans tend to be real prudes when it comes to sex. It never fails that when one dog starts to mount another, humans have a fit, pull the dogs apart, and indicate that they think that this natural act is disgusting. Humans sure are hypocritical about this topic. I came into the family room one day and caught my caregivers doing exactly what they yell at us for doing!

In my travels, I have seen some pretty big dogs – hounds and great Danes – but none can compare to those that Lauren rides, when she and Vince take me out to the stable. These guys are enormous; she calls them horses. Now I don't really mind my trips to the stable because I get to run around with my buddies and chase sticks that the humans throw for us, but when I finish chasing sticks, I just lie in a shady spot while Lauren rides her horse. They go around and around in a circle. I can never see the point of all this. It's not like they actually go anywhere!

At the stable, there is one iron-clad rule: Don't chase the horses! Now that rule is pretty easy for me to follow. Being as perceptive as I am, I know to leave animals bigger than me well alone. It's not that I'm a coward – I just like breathing too much! Well, one of my pals at the stable, Butch, has more barks than smarts. He decides to chase one of the horses out in the paddock, and has a gay old time barking and hounding that poor horse from one end of the paddock to the other. Because there are no humans in sight at the time, I'm sure Butch thought he got away with it. Well, after many sunrises, both Butch and that horse are out in the field. Now Butch apparently forgot all about his transgression, but guess who has not? The horse kind of moseys up close to Butch; then, in a flash, two hind legs lash out. Fortunately for Butch, he only receives a glancing blow. He goes yelping for all he's worth into the stable. From now on, he won't go anywhere near a horse. Some of my canine friends just have to learn the hard way!

Now I do want to make it clear that Vince, Alice and I do love each other dearly. I can have the worst day possible, and, when they come home, they are always glad to see me. They drop whatever they have in their hands and hold and pet me. They always feed me and take me out before they eat. They really are dears!

I want to end my saga with a poem that summarizes how humans should view their canine friends.

We Have a Lot to Learn from Our Dogs

Under the category of 'If only I had known,'
If you are lonely, dogs are the perfect way to meet people.
No matter how different we are,
Dog walkers always have a common bond.
If you are looking for love,
Dogs give more opportunities than dating sites.
We have a lot to learn from our dogs.

My dog has a great 'sniffer'. I say he is reading the morning newspaper.
A fellow dog walker says, "He is reading his pee-mail."
I once got down on all fours, put my nose to the ground to see what I was missing.
I didn't smell anything, but I sure got some looks as two elderly women gave me a wide berth.
I was able to train my dog in a few months. He absolutely will not do his business in the house.
But most men spray bathrooms to varying degrees when trying to pee, before getting their aim.
We have a lot to learn from our dogs.

Most dogs are straight forward. Unlike humans they don't lie.
You know exactly what they think of you. Baring teeth and ears back, watch out! Tail wag, okay.
But like humans the occasional one with sneak behind your back and bite you.

Unlike us, dogs have a very pragmatic view of geopolitics. terrorism and the environment.
Dogs reason, if I mistreat someone, why would he give me some food?
If I screw up the water, what am I going to drink?
If I dump toxic waste everywhere, where am I going to go for my walks?
We indeed have a lot to learn from our dogs.

Vince: *I know it was wrong, but I couldn't help opening Shakespeare's file. My curiosity just got the better of me. After all, it is MY computer, I say to myself, trying to justify my actions.*

I'm quite touched by Shakespeare's words about us caregivers. But, more than that, I realize that his literary skills far outpace my own. His writing has wit, freshness, and honesty that I know I can never equal. Not only does his prose show literary genius, but he is also a masterful poet. He starts this story with a Haiku poem that summarizes how his writing defies the critics, and he ends his story with a free verse that nicely puts us humans in our place. Wow!

An idea suddenly strikes me. Why not have Shakespeare ghostwrite for me in exchange for something he really likes, such as doggie snacks. I'll pretend to be writing from his point of view. Nobody will suspect because everyone knows dogs can't learn English, let alone type out a story – Ha! Ha! This idea is genius!

Shakespeare is hesitant, partly because he is still angry with me for invading his privacy. It will be an arrangement made in heaven if I can only get his consent. I will take his file, put my name on it, and submit it to the publisher. Then I'll be on my way to fame and fortune, and he'll get his pick of any doggy snacks in the pet store!

Shakespeare: *I always get the ultimate word. If Vince now knows that I cognize English and can type on the computer keyboard, then he should also comprehend that I can read; I'm on to his nefarious scheme. A few doggy snacks, in exchange for ghostwriting, is not sufficient for my arduous endeavors. I want remuneration, in proper currency. He should surely realize that if I've mastered English, typing and reading, I can be equally adept at retail. I want payment in cold, hard cash for my ghostwriting, and then I can do my own shopping. Choice is a wonderful thing!*

P.S. Vince – you may have designs on my story, but I hope you appreciate I've also written it in voice, all ready for a stage play...at my namesake theatre in Stratford, perhaps? Of course, I would play the lead role.

Vince: *Shakespeare is a world class bargainer. Governments should hire him for their trade negotiations. He can be ruthless and relentless. The only way I can afford him is if he reduces his monetary demands in exchange for co-authorship of this book. In addition, he insists on the final say on content. He says that he can't trust my judgement on such matters when his reputation as an author is at stake. I can't possibly compete with his giant brain!*

Shakespeare: *I always get the last word. Vince may think I am an indurate arbitrator, but I am in fact quite easy; he evokes pity in me. I am actually quite avuncular towards Vince; however, for me to even consider his proposal I insist that Vince buys me my own computer; one with an enlarged keyboard so my paws don't keep hitting the wrong keys. In addition, I must take over the editing duties since he is obviously so incompetent. In spite of his ineptitude, I enjoy watching Vince play Dr. Watson to my Sherlock Holmes. My prognostication is that the timing for publishing our masterpiece is propitious. I do, however, note that Vince fails to take my thespian hint, but this idea will be dealt with by me after our book is in print.*

Vince: *I know you're a genius, but you don't have to keep using those big words no one understands.*

Shakespeare: *Are you accusing me of being supercilious.*

Vince: *There you go again!*

Shakespeare: *Frankly, I am a little disappointed that a Ph.D. graduate would not have a better command of the English language. Perhaps if you read more instead of watching that thing you call a television, you would be better edified.*

Vince: *What really worries me now is that when you write your next stories, people won't understand your words.*

Shakespeare: *If you had perused my first tale carefully, you would notice that I restricted my vocabulary to words that even the plebeian masses can understand. Anyway, as jocular as this banter is, I must get to work on my next tale for our book.*

Shakespeare hard at work
Notice his concentration on his next tale,
"Buddy's Dilemma."

Tale Two: Buddy's Dilemma

Buddy
Photograph by Laura Morris (used with permission)

Shakespeare: *My next tale has its inception in the Easy Living Rest Home. I tell Vince that we are so fortunate for our situation and should give back to the community. It's easy to discern how even complete strangers are gratified when stroking my fur and petting me. They keep telling Vince how I remind them of a time when they or a relative of theirs had a collie and how wonderful that memory is. I thus instruct Vince to enroll me as a service dog to visit retirement homes. To effectuate this goal, I first must pass an obedience test. It is an unnecessary indignity for me! I understand exactly what to do and can easily accomplish it, but I decide the rules are the rules no matter how inane they are and go along with them. Of course, I pass easily and even coach the other dogs on what the humans want them to do. Some listen and pass; some don't and fail, but what can you do? Sporting my new service jacket, Vince and I enter the Easy Living Rest Home. While he is filling out some paper work before our visit, I notice another collie resting, stretched out on a mat. I introduce myself, and he replies that his name is Buddy. "How come you are here?" I ask. He tells me the most fascinating story that, with his permission, I relate now in his voice.*

Chapter One: Buddy and Sweet

Sweet found her Buddy.
They will never be parted.
But what of Lovely?

BLACK TERROR, THAT'S WHAT IT IS. One minute I'm snuggled next to Mom; then a hand grabs me and thrusts me into a bag. I'm carried for a while and then thrown; I land with a bump. All of a sudden a noise starts, and I'm jostled around for a long time. After we stop, a hand grabs me out of the bag and throws me into some bushes. The big box with wheels that brought me then departs very fast and leaves me alone, all alone. I'm surrounded by all kinds of strange noises that are so scary. I don't like them and whimper, "Where is Mama? I'm so alone!" I see a faint light in the distance and start to scramble towards it; my legs are short, so it takes me a while to get there. As the light becomes brighter, I see it comes from an old farm house that stands by itself in a field. I scramble up to the porch and start to whimper. No one responds, so I crawl under it, curl up in a ball and finally fall asleep.

The next morning, I wake up to noises above me and start to cry as loud as I can. There are sounds of footsteps and then a kind voice. A hand reaches under the porch and lifts me up. A female human cuddles and caresses me. She warms me in her arms and takes me into the house. She has a wrinkled face, but her eyes are bright, and she has broad shoulders. She takes me into a room she calls a kitchen, gives me some food to eat that tastes so good and also puts some water in a dish. I decide to name her Sweet because she is so kind. She gets a basket and puts a pillow in it as I lick her hand. She puts me into it and gives me a pet and a treat. I sit there watching as Sweet works in the kitchen. As she talks to me, she washes dishes at a place she refers to as a sink. Then we play with a pole that has a bundle of straw at its end that Sweet uses to sweep the floor. I attack this pole, grabbing it with my teeth and shaking it. At first Sweet looks cross and utters some angry words. I'm puzzled and think, *Aren't we playing a game?* Then Sweet just shakes her head and laughs. She gives up, pours a liquid into a cup for herself, picks me up, and then we go outside and sit in a chair. Sweet keeps laughing and petting me. She then gives me a hug. After a while we go back into the house, and Sweet once again gets her sweeping device. I think, *Oh boy, we get to play again.* But she shuts me in the kitchen. After whining a bit, I finally give up, snuggle with the pillow in my bed and go to sleep. I'm awakened by Sweet working in the kitchen. She prepares a plate for herself and gives me my food. We both eat, and Sweet once again washes the dishes. She then puts me out on my own in a fenced-in yard. All the new smells are very enjoyable. After I relieve myself, Sweet comes out to me and pets me. She talks to me with a bunch of kind words. She then gives me a treat. I gather that doing my business outside is something that pleases Sweet, so I try to do that from now on. Continuing my sniffing, I suddenly notice through a crack in the fence some huge black and white horned animals in the adjacent field. Their scent is very strange. They start to move towards me, so I rush back to the house in terror. My little legs get tangled in the grass, and I tumble head-over-heels. I pick myself up and ramble to the back door. Sweet is there laughing; she picks me up, and we go into the safety of the kitchen.

That night Sweet puts me into my bed in the kitchen, but she leaves the door open. It is dark, and I hear scary, creaking noises. It's so frightening, I run to the foot of the stairs and whimper loudly. Sweet comes down, pats me, puts me in my bed and goes back upstairs. I then run to the stairs and cry in a determined manner. Once again Sweet comes down, and puts me in my bed before she goes back upstairs. This process is repeated several times before I wear Sweet out, and she picks up both my bed and me and goes upstairs. She puts me in my bed, but I still am scared and start to whine. Finally, Sweet completely gives in with a sleepy nod and takes me into bed with her. I cuddle up to her and at last feel safe and secure. I don't know if she realizes it, but she has just committed to a life-long sleeping companion.

In the morning, Sweet puts a leash on me and takes me outside. I think, *Great! She is taking me for a walk.* Instead she puts me in a big moving box. It reminds me of the last time I was put in one of these scary contraptions. I resist getting in and try to squirm out of her arms as, in my panic, I wonder, *Is she going to dump me by the side of the road?* But then my fear lessens as I realize, *No! This is Sweet. She would never do such a thing!* I relax and let her put me in the front seat where I snuggle next to her, and we drive off. After quite a while, we stop at a building and go inside. Several other dogs are there. It looks like Sweet has brought me here for a play time romp, but the dogs are all on leashes and most don't seem interested in playing. One of them even growls at me when I try to say hello to him by smelling his butt. There is one blond dog with a long tail and floppy ears that is receptive to my greeting, and we touch noses after smelling each other. Finally, a human behind a desk calls out to us, and Sweet takes me into a room. A lady in a white coat then comes in and talks to Sweet for a while. White Coat then picks me up and places me on a table. She puts a disk on my chest that has long tubes that go up to her ears. She smiles and pats me. After looking me all over, she gets some short tubes with sharp points on them. I get scared, but Sweet's pats relax me. Then White Coat stabs me several times. I yelp in protest, but then it's over. Sweet smiles and gives me a biscuit that smells like meat. I sniff it and take a bite. It tastes yummy, so I gobble it. I'm not certain about this place. Little do I know that later, my life will be saved here.

Shakespeare: *I ask my canine friend if he has ever met any other humans except Sweet. He says he also met a girl he calls Lovely because she is so kind to him and loves him so much. I ask him how he met her, and he says she is from Sweet's extended pack. When I ask if he loves her as much as Sweet, he says I'll just have to wait 'till he gets to that part of the story. I think he just enjoys keeping me in suspense!*

Chapter Two: Heroic Buddy

WHEN I BECOME OLDER AND BIGGER, Sweet takes me to another place that also has a room full of dogs. There are all kinds of dogs here: tan dogs with floppy ears, black dogs with short hair and pointed ears, big white dogs with drooping jowls. When I first come in with Sweet, my fellow dogs and I run around sniffing each other to get acquainted. Some of the dogs are shy and cower away from me, but most romp around and just want to play. One dog snarls when I get close and backs away towards his owner.

Finally, a man who does not have a white coat comes out and blah, blah, blahs to the humans who then use our leashes to line us up against a wall. He then brings out a dog that works with him. He utters "blah" and holds a treat over the dog's head; the dog sits and gets the treat. Sweet and the other humans then try the same thing. This trick is pretty easy for me and some of the other dogs, and our handlers only have to teach us once. The others must repeat this process many times before they figure it out. At first I think, *Boy are these dogs dense.* But then it occurs to me, *Hey, they're getting many more treats than me, since they get treats every time their handlers try to teach them to sit. Maybe it's me that's stupid.* I keep that in mind for the rest of our training. This process is repeated for other commands. Each time I decide to play ignorant to maximize my treats. I learn fast.

In our next class, we learn to go to our humans and hold our position despite some distractions such as squeaking toys and a chair that rolls around on wheels. I don't mind because there is always food involved. In our last lesson, we learn to walk beside our humans. I love this because it eventually leads to Sweet and me trekking through the woods.

Our time together during our rambles is spent exploring nature, and Sweet always has a big smile on her face. Sweet picks up sticks and tosses them for me to fetch. When we come to a stream, I jump in for a swim. The cool water feels so good after the dust from the trail. When I get out and shake water all over, Sweet runs away shrieking, but she always comes back laughing. We have great fun together; she is so dear to me. On the way back from a romp through the woods, we pass one of Sweet's pastures where she keeps these big white animals wearing lots of curly wool. They *Baa* a greeting to us, and Sweet waves in response. Obviously, they mean a lot to her.

Then one day as we pass, intruders break through a distant fence. Their images grow larger and larger as they race towards the wooly animals. Finally, fierce looking dogs come into view. Sweet yells and starts to run through the gate and into the field. I can't let these monsters harm Sweet and her friends. I bound through the gate in full attack mode. I pass Sweet and reach the first beast with murder in his eyes, just as he grabs one of the woolies. I bite his flank and scratch at him. He drops Woolie and howls in pain. His companions then arrive and attack me, biting my flanks and neck. The pain is intense. Then there's a loud bang, and one of the beasts falls over. Sweet is running towards me with a long tube at the end of a wooden handle she always carries on our walks. She stops, and there is another loud blast and again one of my attackers falls to the ground, while the others scatter and run for their lives. Then all goes black.

When I wake up. shapes are visible, but they are out of focus. My head is spinning, and I feel woozy. Gradually I recognize Sweet. She's gently holding me. White Coat is also here. She puts her disc connected to long tubes on my chest and smiles. She and Sweet look happy, so everything seems to be all right. They put me in a cage with a soft bed inside. Sweet stays by me just outside my enclosure. I feel sore all over, but after White Coat pricks me, the pain lessens. Now I just want to go to sleep. Every day is better until finally Sweet takes me home where we can snuggle in bed. A while later we begin our walks again. At first, we take it slow, but after a few weeks I feel more like my old self. It is so much fun to once again race through the woods and chase little brown four-legged animals that scurry up trees. They always elude me. To tell the truth, I'm not sure what would happen if I did catch one, but the chase is fun. It makes Sweet laugh when I stand by the tree and bark and try to look so tough.

One day Sweet is very busy in the kitchen. All kinds of great smells emerge from there. I'm especially interested in a big platter of meat that's just out of my reach and makes me salivate. Later in the morning the doorbell starts to ring, and people flood into the front room. *Could they all be from Sweet's pack, since she hugs and kisses them?* I greet them with a wagging tail. Some come right up to me and pet me, but some are more *stand-offish* despite my best efforts to be friendly. The children are the best. They hug me and rub my fur. One little girl that I call Lovely is especially sweet, hence her name. She just wants to hug me and pet me all the time. Licking her results in squeals of delight. After a while everyone goes outside and sits at big tables that some of the men set up outside. I lie down right by Lovely. Every once in a while, she slips me some meat from her plate. It tastes so yummy. No one notices because everyone is busy talking; this gathering is loud and happy. At the end of the meal, Lovely sneaks me something that tastes sweet. It's probably not good for me, but I don't care. It tastes so delicious. After everyone eats, Lovely pleads with Sweet and a woman, who is probably her mother. Finally, Sweet and the lady both nod, and Lovely attaches a leash to my collar. We then set out for a walk. We enter the coolness of the forest following a path that is familiar to me. Finally, we come to the river where I sometimes swim, but today the water level is high, and the current is swift. Lovely takes off her shoes and socks, rolls up her pants and starts to wade into the water. I sense danger and bark a warning, but it's too late. The current catches her and knocks her off balance. She screams as the force of the water drags her away from the bank. I jump into the raging torrent and grab Lovely by the collar just as her head disappears below the water. I pull her head up and paddle with all my strength towards the shore. Just when it seems I can swim no more, we reach the bank. I use the last of my energy to pull us up on the shore. I lie on the bank panting while Lovely is coughing and gasping for air. As we recover, Lovely hugs me so tight I can hardly breathe. She even laughs when I shake water all over her. When we arrive back home, everyone comes running toward us. I assume Lovely tells them what happened because they all crowd around and give me pats and hugs despite my still being wet. Even the *stand-offish* ones join in. Later, as everyone is leaving, Lovely hugs me until her mother pulls her away. She cries and extends her hands out to me while Sweet holds my leash so I can't go to her. I'm sad when Lovely leaves, but it's wonderful to snuggle extra close to Sweet that night. The next morning, Sweet gives me a long hug and feeds me some meat off her plate, which she normally never does. As we sit on the front porch she laughs as I jump up and snap at a little thing that flies right by my mouth. I lie back down and Sweet pets me while she hums a melody. Her touch makes me so happy. We have a love that we speak to each other in a silent language that we both understand.

Chapter Three: Buddy in Service

AFTER SEVERAL MORE SNOW FALLS, Sweet takes me in her big moving box with wheels, and we go to a room where there are other dogs. However, unlike before, these dogs are all older and are very serious. A man and a woman come out and start to go "blah, blah, blah" to the human dog handlers. Then we all line up, and the man barks out a word I understand, "*Sit.*" Most of us do sit, but a few don't. The thought of playing dumb crosses my mind, but Sweet looks very serious and I don't want to disappoint her. One dog just won't sit, so he and his human leave. The dog doesn't seem too upset, but his human looks very sad and has tears in her eyes. The man then comes around and pats all of us. A few of the remaining dogs get up as soon as he touches them, and their humans must have them sit again and start the whole process all over. When it's my turn, the sadness of the owner whose dog failed flashes in my mind, so I remain motionless. I don't ever want to make Sweet cry. We then have to walk around a bunch of boxes with treats on them, but we aren't allowed to have them no matter how tempting they are. A few dogs just can't resist and after failing this test many times, they also have to leave. Finally, the man sits in a chair on wheels, and the woman walks supported by a stick. They go all around us to see what we will do. The man in the chair pats me and chatters at me. I'm tempted to run, but when Sweet nods to me in assurance, I'm okay and stay put. A few of the dogs bark and bite at the chair and stick; that's all for them – they're gone.

Glancing up at Sweet, I see such a look of relief and pride in her face; I guess everything is alright. All the dogs that are left, including me, each get a jacket put on us by our humans. I don't really like it but will do anything for Sweet; she seems so happy when she puts it on me. Sweet then gets a piece of paper, and we go home where Sweet gives me lots of my favorite treats. It is so wonderful.

The significance of what I've accomplished and the jacket isn't clear, until one day when Sweet puts my jacket on me, and we ride to a huge building. After entering the building, Sweet takes me to the front desk where she shows a paper and my jacket to a woman. Then we go into a little room with no windows. Sweet pushes a button, and the door slides shut. I can feel us moving up. I'm a little scared and press against Sweet who gives me a reassuring pat. After the little room stops its motion, the door opens, and we enter a corridor with lots of rooms. There are many people walking around with sticks. Some others are in chairs with wheels. They all watch intently as we walk by them. We then go into a huge room where people are sitting and watching a large box with moving, flashing lights. Many have wrinkled faces and gray hair, like Sweet; some have no hair at all. They all look towards us as we enter the room. One woman rushes over to us and hugs me. She utters a sound that Sweet sometimes says when referring to me, "*Collie.*" The rest of the people walk and hobble over to me and gently pet me. There is one man on the couch, I call Solitary, who doesn't join them. I go over to him and put my head in his lap. Looking into his eyes, there is real pain and sorrow. He remains motionless for a long time.

Then in a slow and deliberate manner, he puts his hand on my head and pats me. Tears form in his eyes, and he begins to weep as he puts his head against mine. He then kisses the top of my head. I remain with him for a long time, and everyone crowds around us. When Sweet finally pulls on my collar, signaling that it is time to leave, there is real joy and love in her face. That makes me so happy. As we walk down the corridor, I notice an old, frail woman staring out of the window in her room, all alone. I pull on my leash as we go by, so we can visit her. As I approach the woman, I name Forlorn, she turns and sees me. Her face suddenly brightens, and she starts to pat the air. Going right up to her, she embraces me and strokes my fur. She seems to yearn for my company. We spend a long time in her room, but finally Sweet tugs on my leash as a sign we must be on our way. It's sad to leave the lady, but I feel certain that Sweet will bring me back here again.

We do make many trips to this building. We always stop to see Forlorn in her room. She always beams and pats the air until she can pet me. I always look forward to seeing her, but one day her room is empty. We never see her again, but it seems like I brought her some joy.

A person I remember from the hospital courtyard, I call Quivers, shakes and makes funny sounds. The strangest thing happens when I come up to him. As soon as our eyes meet, he stops shaking and sticks out his hand. As he pets my head, he seems much calmer, and I perceive some cheer in his face. Someone else I enjoy seeing is a lady who always gives me something tasty from a bag. When this woman, I call Treats, gives them to me, she gets the biggest grin on her face. Her delicacies are always a welcome bonus to the happiness our visits give me. I don't know at the time how much of a pull this place will have on me.

Chapter Four: Buddy's Choice

SWEET AND I CELEBRATE MANY more visits from her pack. Each time, Lovely runs and hugs me. She still slips some meat to me at dinner. We take many walks together, but we always are careful to avoid the river. It's so much fun to romp and play with her. With time, Lovely changes; she is taller and more adult looking. But her scent is the same, so she is always recognizable to me no matter how different her appearance is. I also notice that Sweet is changing. She now bends over a little when she walks and is not so spry. Our walks become slower and shorter. On our last walk, something strange and terrifying happens. Our walk starts as usual. Sweet clicks my leash on my collar, and we set out. Once we reach the woods, a look appears on Sweet's face that I have never seen before. She appears scared and lost. She doesn't seem to know where we are, even though we have stood on this spot many times. Sweet drops my leash and rushes from tree to tree in a panic. She grabs onto each one for support and has a wild look on her face. Then Sweet starts to run deeper into the forest, and I race after her. She trips over a root where it emerges from the ground and tumbles into a pile of leaves. She curls up into a ball, and her shoulders heave as she breaks the silence of the forest with her sobs. I rush to her side and nuzzle her with my nose. Suddenly she grabs onto my neck with both her hands and hugs me. After a long while, she sits up with a more controlled look. In our silent language, she signals to me that she is okay now. Sweet then struggles to her feet, takes my leash, and I lead her home. We never go out on our long walks again. I don't mind too much because I don't ever want to see Sweet so scared. Also, I don't have the energy I once had and just enjoy resting by Sweet.

Things are fine for a while, but one day Sweet forgets to feed me my morning meal. She comes downstairs as usual and goes into the kitchen. I see her put some black powder into a container. She then pours water into the pot as usual and plugs a long black cord into the wall. As the pot starts to perk, she breaks some white roundish things, and a clear liquid with a yellow circle flows into a pan. Sweet then turns some knobs on a big white object in the kitchen. It's now she usually gets out my food, but she does not pour anything into my bowl. I whine a little, but she just pats me and goes on humming while she stirs the things in the pan. After she eats, Sweet attaches my leash and takes me out to the front lawn for me to do my business. She doesn't respond to my whimpers throughout the day. I'm trying to signal that I missed my meal, but she doesn't seem to get my hints. She just pats me; I believe she thinks she's already fed me. I don't understand but don't ever want to upset Sweet, so I finally just accept that this meal will be missed. Fortunately, she does remember to give me my evening meal, which I gobble up, since I'm famished. After this episode, my meals begin to become more and more erratic. Sometimes I get two morning meals and none at night or vice-versa. Occasionally. I get no meals all day long. Also, sometimes Sweet even forgets to feed herself. I become more and more worried about her, but I don't know what to do. Finally, things come to a head one day when the doorbell rings. I go downstairs to see who's there. Sweet doesn't come down with me. The sunlight through the windows is now quite bright, and my stomach tells me the time for my morning meal has long since passed.

When Sweet doesn't respond to the door bell, someone starts knocking on the door, which quickly turns into pounding. I become very concerned and start barking. All of a sudden, amid all this confusion, I hear a stirring from upstairs, and Sweet descends the stairs in her night dress. She opens the door to reveal Lovely and her pack on the porch with anxious looks on their faces. They converse for a long time. Lovely and other members of the pack look very disquiet, and Sweet appears quite befuddled. Then while Lovely kneels by me and starts to pet me, the pack starts to look around the house. I know that often Sweet does not put things where they usually belong, and she spends a lot of time looking for things. I try to help her by showing her what I think she's looking for. I hear some noise from the kitchen and go in just as one of the pack members turns off a flame from a burner on the stove. Everyone gathers around with worry on their faces. Sweet just looks puzzled and wanders out of the room. Lovely rushes after her, brings her back and seats her in a chair. Lovely and I stay with Sweet while the others go into a front room. I can hear blah, blah, blahs for a long time. Finally, one of the pack comes back into the kitchen and talks with Lovely. She nods and starts to fix some food for Sweet and me, while the others leave. Lovely stays with us all day and night. The next morning, all of Sweet's pack gathers at her house. They start to pack up some of Sweet's things. I don't know what's going on and rush to Sweet who pets me, but when I look into her eyes, I don't see a sign of recognition. When Sweet's pack starts to lead her out of her door and into one of the big boxes on wheels, I try to go with her. The pack shakes their heads, and one of them blah, blah, blahs to Lovely. She disappears inside the house and comes out with my leash. She then clicks it onto my collar and holds me. The big box pulls away with Sweet inside, and I howl and start to follow. Lovely keeps a firm grip on my leash and pulls me back. *I have to go with Sweet. She needs me.* I wonder, *Why won't they let me go to her?* After Sweet has gone, Lovely takes me into another big box with wheels. I think, *Maybe Lovely is going to take me to see Sweet.* We end up at Lovely's house, which I recognize from previous times Sweet and I visited her. Once inside I run to every room looking for Sweet, but neither she nor her scent are here. I go to the door and scratch to go out, so I can find Sweet, but Lovely brings me back into a front room, and looks at me with sympathetic and loving eyes. I begin to understand that she is telling me that she will be my mistress from now on.

This is where my great conflict begins. Lovely devotes herself to me. When I look into her eyes, they are filled with love. She brushes and cuddles me. She not only feeds me my regular food, but she gives me the yummiest treats. We go on long walks and romp in a park with green grass and trees, just like I use to frolic with Sweet. *Oh Sweet! How I long for you. Do you need me? Do you miss me? Oh, I love you so much.* But Lovely is so kind. I can't leave her and break her heart. As I lie in bed next to sleeping Lovely, I ponder all the kindness she has shown me. Then a picture of Sweet flashes into my mind. I remember how she saved me. How she filled my heart with love. *Is she all alone? Is she weeping? Can I help her?* My course of action then becomes clear to me. I hope Lovely will understand and forgive me, but Sweet needs me to take care of her. I must be there for her the same way she was always there for me, but I must bide my time and can never leave while Lovely is watching. It's cowardly of me, but if she starts to cry, I can't go. My chance comes one day when Lovely and her pack go somewhere in their box with wheels and leave me tied up on the porch. As Lovely puts down a water dish for me, I bow my head in shame and feel I am betraying her love and trust. Once they leave, I start to work, chewing on my leather leash. I finally chew it down to the point where it snaps with one good tug. Reaching the end of the road leading to Lovely's home, I go in the direction of the only place I can think Sweet may be, the place where we always went to visit people who are like Sweet is now. As I walk down the road, I must be careful of boxes with wheels, which go roaring by. After a long while, I feel very thirsty and stop by a muddy pool of water. Compared to the crystal-clear water I'm used to, it tastes awful, but my thirst makes me gulp it anyway.

As darkness comes, I stop by a farm house. I'm famished, and a big metal can emits the most tempting odors. When I tip it over, it clangs with a terrible racket, that scares me. I dash away, but the smell quickly draws me back. Just as I grab a bone a door creaks open, and a man is shouting. He raises a long tube, and the ground beside me explodes in a hail of gravel that stings me. As I run for my life, another loud boom blasts out. I don't stop until the house is out of sight, and the man is not chasing me. I lie down on some tall grass, drop my bone that I managed to hang onto during my ordeal and start to lick where the little stones hit me. My tongue then licks my sore and tired feet. Only then do I start to chew on the bone. It tastes so good and renews some of my strength. I then curl up in a ball and finally fall asleep.

When I wake up, going back to Lovely seems very appealing. With her there is lots of fresh water, good food, and no exploding rocks hitting me. In fact, I do start back toward Lovely's house, but then Sweet's face appears to me. She's calling me, and there is no forsaking her. So I turn around and continue on my quest. The sun sets and rises several times more on my journey. Then my goal comes into sight. Despite the pain from my torn and bleeding feet, I rush towards it. By the time I reach the grass surrounding the building, I am limping badly. It's all I can do to reach the entrance where I collapse, but there is a familiar scent. Can it be? Yes, it belongs to Sweet.

As I lie there, a woman in white come running towards me. She kneels by me and then yells something. I recognize her as someone who used to always greet Sweet and me when we came to visit. Then a man comes and lays me on a blanket that the lady in white puts down. The man gets some water that I manage to lap up a little. The lady in white then cleans my feet and rubs them with a cloth that has something on it that stings and makes me flinch, but she pets my head and sooths me. She then wraps my feet in some white strips as I lick her in gratitude. I try to get up to find Sweet, but they won't let me. Finally, I give into my exhaustion and fall asleep.

When I wake up, Lovely's tear-stained face is there. She looks at me with a doleful, questioning gaze and then hugs and kisses me. I'm so happy to see her that I lick her face. Then a man starts to pick me up and take me towards the door. No! I have to see Sweet, to be with her. I struggle out of his arms, land with a thump and stagger towards Sweet's scent. Lovely comes after me, crying. Finally, I see a look of understanding in her face. She calls to the lady in white and has a long talk with her. The lady nods and then goes into the little room with the buttons and sliding door. Later she emerges with my Sweet in a chair with wheels. I bark with joy and rush to her as fast as I can manage. She hugs me and strokes my fur while I lick her face. All my trials and hardships are forgotten. We're both transfixed with the total joy of this moment.

While Sweet and I continue our happiness, the others stand around in a circle. Finally, Lovely takes Sweet and me into the little room with the buttons and sliding door. When we get out, we go into a room with a bed. Sweet's scent is very strong here, so I assume it's her room. Thus, I spend many happy days and nights here with Sweet. Some mornings she calls out my name and seems to recognize me and sometimes she does not, but that doesn't matter. She pets me, and I lick her regardless. Lovely comes to visit us often. One time she comes with a man and a tiny human. When I sniff the little human, he smells like Lovely and faintly like Sweet. I can't imagine being happier.

Vince: *I tell Shakespeare's that this will surely be one of his most touching tales. It demonstrates the value of the collaboration of Shakespeare and me. Only another dog could tell this story of devotion and love with such understanding and emotion.*
Shakespeare: *I just hope that this tale encourages humans to use dogs to help the neglected and lonely people that are too often shut away and forgotten.*
Vince: *I've often admired Shakespeare for his intellect and genius, but his telling of this story also shows how much love and compassion for others he has in his heart. I've never been so proud to be associated with him.*

Tale Three: Cuddles

Cuddles
(Photo credit: Top Photo Engineer/Shutterstock)

Shakespeare: *Dogs and cats have a long-standing feud. Personally, I view this situation as juvenile and inane. I think, If only I could converse in Cat, perhaps I could dispel some of the altercations that seem to plague us. So, I start observing cats' unique forms of communication. At first this has to be done at a distance, but as I gain more proficiency in their language, I convince a few cats that I am not churlish and only want to learn from them. I appeal to their vanity and tell them, as an inferior species, I want to be edified by them and educate my fellow canines not to chase them. I am aware that my brain is far superior to any cat's and that to imply otherwise is a prevarication, but it is one that is expedient. This ruse seemed to work, and these cats complete my education on speaking fluent Cat.*

Vince is astonished when he finds out that I not only can communicate in exemplary English, but also Cat. I must admit that compared to English, Cat is more arduous and subtle. Cats always seem to have a superior and lofty air about them that is reflected in their language. They are very enigmatic and don't always tell you everything they are thinking. They leave it up to you to "fill in the blanks."

Anyway, this tale begins with a visit we make to Alvin Jones, who is Vince's friend. Vince told me that Alvin is very impressed by the close bond that Vince and I share. However, I'm sure he has no idea of my literary and linguistic talents. He lost his family and went through a "rough patch", but according to Vince, he is much better now thanks to a friend he made, a cat called Cuddles. Since Vince and I formed our partnership, I have always been anxious to explore tales of symbiotic relationships between humans and other animals. Our visit provides a perfect opportunity.

After greeting us, Alvin goes into the kitchen to get some drinks. While he is away, Vince sets up my computer on the floor in an unobtrusive corner where Alvin can't observe me typing. After Alvin comes back, he and Vince sit down. As we have arranged, Vince asks how Cuddles came into his life. Alvin replies that Cuddles saved him after the death of his wife and children. He then elaborates, and I begin to compose, in his voice, his story into a tale, adding a flare for the dramatic where I think it is necessary.

Chapter One: Alvin's Nightmare

All is in darkness.
There is nothing left but death.
But Cuddles saved me.

W*HY? WHY? WHY?* THE QUESTION pounds in my brain like a jackhammer. Everything was so perfect. Susan, with her sweet, adorable face loved me. She was an angel on earth. Our kids, our wonderful, beautiful kids, I can see their innocent eyes staring at me even now. They had been so good. Susan took them out to get some chocolate ice cream – their favorite. Then that phone call! That awful, jarring blare from the phone. The words that ensue are seared into my brain.

"Mr. Jones, Mr. Jones, are you there?"

"Yes, can I help you?" I answer.

"There has been an accident. Can you come to the Parkview Hospital right now, to the emergency room?"

"What...What happened? Is my family alright? Tell me!" I plead.

"I think it's best if you can come right now."

I drive like a crazy man and fly through the emergency-room doors.

"What happened? Tell me! Is my family alright?"

"What's your name?" the woman behind the reception desk asks.

"It's Jones! Alvin Jones! Are they all right? Tell me!"

The woman at the desk looks very grave and replies, "Someone will be with you right away, please have a seat."

She must be kidding; how can I sit? I pace like a caged tiger. Then a young doctor appears.

"Please come with me to the visitors' room Mr. Jones," she says. "It is quiet there, and we can talk without any interruptions."

"Tell me. Tell me what happened!" I demand.

"There has been a terrible accident. The ambulance attendants said a speeding truck hit your car head on. I'm afraid your wife was killed immediately."

"No! Not Susan. Oh my God no!...My kids! What about my kids?"

"They're both here in critical condition. They're in surgery now. They both sustained serious head injuries. I'm so sorry. Is there anyone we can call to come and sit with you?"

"No, there's no one."

"We have a chaplain who could ..."

"No! I don't want anyone...I'm sorry. I just need to be alone right now."

"Well okay, if you are sure... I'll come and find you as soon as we have any news."

I somehow wander into the cafeteria and get a coffee from the vending machine. I mechanically sip it without tasting anything. What is most hateful about hospitals is the waiting, the endless waiting, the helpless waiting. You can do nothing while fate rolls the dice and decides if those you love more than yourself live or die, whether your life will be left with any meaning or become a mechanical existence. After an eternity of waiting and numerous tasteless cups of coffee, the doctor appears with a grim look on her face.

"No, they're not. Tell me they're not dead," I plead.

"I'm sorry Mr. Jones; they both died from head trauma, if only they'd been strapped in with seat belts..."

I thought, *If only our old car had come with seat belts. Why didn't I get them installed as I'd intended? Why didn't I forget about everything else and just do it?* The hell of the next few days is unbearable. Sitting in the funeral home, I feel completely empty and have no more tears to cry. I stand while the white coffins are rolled by – first my wife's and then two small coffins for my children. Why the children? Why could cruel fate not spare just one of my kids? Why not take me instead of them? I would have gladly replaced them.

The whole funeral service experience is surreal. I see everything, but don't hear a word. At the reception, I shake hands like a preprogrammed robot – nodding at all the words of sympathy. My fellow mourners mean well, but none of their words of condolences do any good. They will not bring back my family. When I go home, it's even worse. There are the endless rings of the doorbell. The drill is always the same. Some neighbor or friend hands me a casserole and says how very sorry they are. After they leave, their contribution is added to the stacks of uneaten casseroles that are piling up in the kitchen. I can't eat. I can't sleep. I'm a shell leading a meaningless existence.

Finally, it's not possible to take any more; the guilt and grief are more than is bearable. I go down to the local gun shop, fill out the paper work and purchase a gun. I bring it home, put it on my coffee table and take out pictures of my family. I hold, kiss, and embrace them; time just slips away without my noticing. It turns dark, the wind picks up, and it starts to rain. A thunder clap suddenly brings me back to the present time. I turn the pictures face down. I pick up the gun and load it, bullet by bullet by bullet. I then stare into the barrel, into an empty abyss of eternity. I can feel my finger beginning to tighten around the trigger. I then hear something coming from outside, from my porch. No! I start to focus again on the barrel of the gun. There it is again. I feel compelled to investigate what's making that sound. I don't know what prompts me, maybe it's Susan's spirit.

Shakespeare: *At this point in his narrative, Alvin brakes down. Maybe it's the thought of his family and his contemplation of suicide. Vince pats him on the back and suggests they go into the kitchen to refresh their drinks. When Alvin agrees, it gives me a chance to talk to Cuddles.*
As I approach Cuddles, she starts to shake and backs into a corner, but when I tell her in my best Cat, I only want to get her side of the story, she looks at me with a disbelieving expression, dumbfounded that I can address her in her native language. Finally, I'm able to gain her trust enough to convince her to tell the story from her view point. My tale thus continues in Cuddles's voice.

Chapter Two: Cuddles's Nightmare

LIFE'S GREAT. I CUDDLE UP NEXT to Mom with my brothers and sisters. It's so cozy and warm, and Mom gives us lots of milk to keep our tummies full. She even knows where to lick us, so we can relieve ourselves. The only time we're alone is when Mom goes out hunting to catch some food; she must keep her strength up as we are hungry kids. When she's away, we are quite still, especially when the four-legged devils are around.

Mom says, "These monsters are fierce, have very powerful jaws, and hate cats; they would tear you all to shreds."

When we are old enough to leave our den and can wander around a little with Mom at night, she also warns us about something else that is just as dangerous as the four-legged devils. She calls them two-eyed monsters. She says,

"These monsters are much bigger and faster than the four-legged devils. They don't have teeth but move on round objects and can crush you to death. At night their eyes glow bright and blind you. While you freeze with fear, they crush you."

One night, Mom's away hunting; my brothers, sisters and I are all snuggled up together. Suddenly, we see an animal moving across the way, sniffing at the bushes. It's a four-legged devil. It comes over to our side of the street. We all cringe in fear. It starts to sniff at the bushes close to us. As it begins to rain; a bright light that flashes from the sky reveals its savage teeth. The storm does not deter the devil. It starts to move ever closer, closer, closer. Just as we are ready to scatter for our lives, we hear a call. Someone's yelling something to the four-legged devil. The devil looks in the direction of the voice, which calls out again, but sterner. The devil hesitates and looks once more in our direction and then runs off towards the voice. We're safe, but for how long?

When Mom comes back, we all tell her what happened, and how scared we are. Mom says,

"Even though there's a storm, we all have to move right now. It isn't safe here anymore; the four-legged devil can come back any time."

In a calm and silent manner, she slips out of our hiding place. She motions for us to follow. I'm so frightened that I can't move. Just as she leads the others half way across the road, a two-eyed monster races out from nowhere. Mom's frozen by its glaring eyes, and she's run over and crushed as the two-eyed monster speeds off.

"Mommy! Mommy!" my brothers and sisters all cry and poke her motionless body... but she does not move.

Just then a second two-eyed monster speeds into view. My litter mates appear to be blinded by its white, menacing eyes. As the monster speeds by, the final cries of my brothers and sisters pierce my very being. In panic, I run from my hiding spot until exhaustion overtakes me. A light from a porch down the street is now visible. I crawl to it and huddle by a step. It's so very frigid. I cry for my mommy even though I know she can't answer. The freezing cold's engulfing me. A face appears at a slightly-open door; oh, it's gone. I'm too cold and exhausted to move. Then the face is there again, and a hand reaches toward me.

Shakespeare: *Just then Vince and Alvin came back and sit down. I apologize to Cuddles for cutting off her narrative and explained that I must continue with Alvin's story. Being the lady she is, Cuddles doesn't object. Alvin asks where he left off. Vince replies that it's where he heard something by his porch. "Oh, yes" Alvin says, and he continues his story, which I relay in his voice.*

Chapter Three: Alvin Finds Cuddles

WHEN I REACH THE DOOR and peer out, there is this pathetic kitten, who's soaked through. *No, I can't deal with this right now.* I close the door and go back to my gun that's patiently waiting to send me into oblivion, away from the hell, which currently surrounds me. I don't know what happened next. Perhaps Susan's soul speaks to me. *Don't you dare use your grief as an excuse to abandon that poor creature! Gather up any shred of humanity you have left and help!* I heed her chastisement, open the door and gather up the poor, wretched little soul.

I take it into the bathroom and dry it off with a thick, fluffy towel. Then by instinct I put the poor dear under my shirt to let it share my body's warmth. Since I know nothing about kittens, I go to the fount of all knowledge, the internet, to find out how to care for my little charge. It informs me that sharing my body heat is the right thing to do. Apparently young kittens cannot generate their own heat and so wrapping them up in a towel does no good. You must put them next to your skin where they can adsorb your body's heat. The next thing's food. It's a good thing I checked the oracle because, otherwise, I would have done everything wrong. You don't feed a kitten when it's cold, and you do not give it straight cow's milk. I wait until the kitten stops shivering. Then, with the kitten's head just poking out from my shirt, I go into the kitchen to prepare some emergency kitten formula, since all the stores are closed. Whole milk, raw egg yolks, and corn oil are mixed according to the directions on the internet and then warmed to room temperature in the microwave. I then find an old eye dropper and wash it out. If it wasn't for the instructions from my computer, I probably would've choked the poor little thing to death trying to feed it. As I religiously obey the instructions, the kitten starts to lick the formula from the eye dropper. Since the kitten's eyes are open and its ears are up, it's about three weeks old according to the font of wisdom. Therefore, I feed it about every six hours. After the kitten eats, I put it back next to my chest, and then it starts ...the loudest purring I have ever heard. It's mesmerizing and therapeutic. I begin to feel drowsy and drift off to sleep... The alarm clock, that I had set, wakes me up in time for the next feeding, and then I'm lulled back to sleep again by the purring. It's the first time I slept since the accident.

Upon waking up, I feel something furry around my neck. I'm wearing a kitten scarf! What happened last night seems like a dream, but here is the evidence. It's real. I stagger into the kitchen to make a cup of coffee. I once again make the kitten's formula and feed it while drinking my coffee. I then wander into the living room. There's my gun, right where I had left it. I sit down and right the pictures of my family. As the kitten starts its loud purring, I swear my wife is grinning. What I had almost done last night seems inconceivable now. I get up and put the gun into my desk drawer. Sitting down again, I gather up my pictures and introduce the little kitten to my family. I then make an appointment with a vet clinic. Fortunately, they had just received a cancellation and are able to fit us in right away. Because of how much Cuddles means to me, I remember what happened next like it was yesterday.

Entering the vet clinic, I greet the technician,

"Hello. I'm Alvin Jones. I have an appointment for this kitten."

"Yes, we have you listed right here. Would you please fill out this form?"

I oblige and fill out as much as I can.

"Here's the form; I actually just found this kitten by my porch and assume it's a stray. It was in pretty rough shape. You ask for the kitten's name. I'm kind of embarrassed to ask, but can you tell me if it's a boy or a girl."

"That's okay. It can be hard to tell with a kitten." She turns the kitten over and examiners her. She then declares, "It's a girl."

"Well considering that she has continuously cuddled with me ever since I found her, I'll call her Cuddles."

"Good. If you will follow me, you can wait in one of our examination rooms. The vet will be with you shortly."

When the vet comes in, I can't help but be impressed by her warm and friendly smile.

"Hi, I'm Dr. Rachael Barrett, and this must be our patient."

"Yes, I found her by my porch, exhausted and soaking wet from the rain."

"I'm impressed that you took her in. It's shameful how many people won't show compassion for such a small creature. Do you plan on keeping her?"

"Well I'm not sure. I haven't really decided yet."

"I hope you do. The shelters are already filled to capacity with cats. I'm afraid some of them may have to be put to sleep."

"You mean killed. No! I can't allow that. Not after all she has been through."

"Good. You look like a man that needs a kitten."

Just then Cuddles begins to purr in my arms.

"See. She agrees with me. Now let's get on with looking at her."

After the examination, the verdict is that I have a healthy kitten. Cuddles gets all of her shots, and I buy some proper formula and solid food for her, which I'm to introduce slowly. Over the next few months, Cuddles continues to serve as a balm to my fractured soul. She starts to scamper all around and gets into everything. Our favorite time is when we play with a feather on a string. She loves chasing it as I make it dance in all different directions. I still feel an ache in my heart for my lost family and often take their pictures out to kiss them, but I'm now eating and sleeping thanks to Cuddles. I'm also able to go to work but always come back home to check on Cuddles at noon. As the years go by, Cuddles becomes my faithful companion. During the summer, we go outside after I get home from work. While I read the paper, Cuddles goes exploring. One day, Cuddles's rambling leads to an unexpected meeting.

Shakespeare: *Just then the phone rings, and Alvin goes to answer it. I take advantage of the break to ask Cuddles about playing in Alvin's yard and what meeting Alvin is taking about. She replies as follows:*

Chapter Four: Cuddles Makes a New Friend

MY FAVORITE TIME IS WHEN DAD and I go outside together. He sits in a chair and looks at a big piece of paper with funny scribbles on it, while I go on back yard safaris, stalking all kinds of things that seem to scamper or fly just out of my reach. One day while Dad is busy reading, I spot a bird several houses over. I have never been a successful hunter, but this time I'll triumph! I creep closer and closer, staying near to the ground. I'm careful not to step on any twigs that might give away my presence. The closer my prey, the more I zero in on my target. Just as I prepare to spring, the bird spots me and flies up to a branch.

"That's a real bummer. I've been trying to catch that bird ever since my mistress and I moved here."

Turning my head towards the source of the voice, I see a rather handsome, black cat with white feet. As he comes running over, I ask,

"How long have you been here? I haven't seen you before."

"My mistress and I just moved here a short while ago. She's a really neat lady. I get to spend all day at her work, so she sees me often and gives me treats all day. Hey, that pesky bird is now squawking at us up in the tree. He's just daring us to try and get him. Follow me!"

With that, my new friend starts to climb.

"Well, are you coming or not?" he challenges me.

I'm a little afraid, but I start to climb. *Don't look down! Don't look down*! I think. When I reach the top of the trunk, I find myself in a 'V'- shaped notch as branches extend up in both directions. My friend's climbing out onto smaller and smaller branches, trying to reach the bird. Just as he reaches the branch that holds the bird, it soars off. He then finds that he can't turn around. I'm also stuck and can't go up or down. We're trapped! Both of us start to cry with all our might.

Shakespeare: *Alvin then returns and declares to Vince, "That was my neighbor Rachael; She's coming over as soon as she picks up some food for her cat, Boots. She says that after all I've told her about you and Shakespeare, she has to meet you. While we're waiting, I guess I should complete my story. Let's see, yes Cuddles and I are in the back yard... "*

Chapter Five: Alvin Finds Happiness

AS I START TO TURN THE PAGE of my newspaper, I notice that Cuddles is not in the yard. I then hear a ruckus and some loud mewing in a neighbor's yard. As I run over, I see Cuddles and another cat up in a tree. Behind me I hear someone calling,

"Boots come on down."

Turning around, I'm surprised to see it's the vet who tended to Cuddles. Her words still ring in my head.

"Oh, it's Alvin, Alvin Jones isn't it? I remember you from the vet clinic. I'm Rachael Barrett,"

"Yes, I recall. We both seem to have the same problem. I'll get my ladder"

I find the ladder in my garage, prop it up against the tree, climb up and grab Cuddles. I then hand her down to Rachael. Boots is too far up the tree for me to reach, so I have to climb up the tree from the ladder.

"Ouch," I scrape my arm on a branch. I climb higher, reach out and grab Boots. He digs into my hand with his claws, but I'm in such a precarious position I can't pull him free. As I'm climbing down, I almost slip, further scratching myself and drawing a gasp from Rachael. When I hand Boots to Rachael, she thanks me and rewards me with a hug and a kiss on my cheek.

"Oh thank you. You're so brave," she gushes; "You're hurt," she observes. "You have to come inside and let me bandage your arm and hand. I don't want your wounds to get infected." We go into her kitchen and she says. "Sit here, and let me take care of you," as she gets out some antiseptic from a first aid kit. As she applies it, she says, "This may sting a bit."

I don't really mind; all I can think about is what a beautiful smile she has. As she is bandaging me, I notice she has coal black hair, which sets off her fair complexion. Her doe-like brown eyes are inviting pools into which you can fall. I snap back to the present moment when she asks,

"Is it just you and Cuddles at home?"

"Err...Yes, I lost my wife and kids several years ago."

"I'm so sorry about your family. I didn't realize."

"That's okay. You had no way of knowing. How about you?"

"I'm alone with Boots. I guess I was too busy with my studies, at university and vet college, to ever meet anyone."

"Well it's their loss," I say as Rachael blushes a little. I have a feeling that Cuddles and I will be spending quite a bit of time over at Rachael's house.

"You know, when I first met you, what really impressed me was how you saved Cuddles," says Rachael.

"Well it's great I made a good first impression, but what you're saying is not quite accurate. I didn't save Cuddles as much as we saved each other!"

Shakespeare: *Just as Alvin ends his story, the doorbell rings. It's Rachael and Boots. A light beams in Alvin's eyes as soon as he sees her. I can tell that Alvin doesn't just owe his life to Cuddles, but also his happiness!*

Vince: *I love this story, but it leaves me with one question. I know your tolerant nature allows you to write a story where a cat is the hero, but I'm surprised that you have a dog as a villain. Shakespeare's answer surprises me.*

Shakespeare: *Just like humans, not all dogs are the same. Some are kind and gentle and others can be mean and cruel. For both humans and dogs, a lot of their behavior can be attributed to how they were raised. You've only shown me kindness and love, so of course that affects my personality and view point.*

Vince: *I'm quite touched by his words. I'm also quite impressed by the depth of understanding he exhibits about development of behavior and personality traits. Shakespeare once again demonstrates his genius.*

Tale Four: Zing's Gift

Zing and Lauren

Ready to do battle at a competition

Shakespeare: *Vince has a lot of stories about his family that he wants to convey, but sadly, he lacks the talent to do so. That is where I come in. He relates his stories to me, and I convert them into interesting prose that people want to read. One of the stories he has related to me I find particularly touching.*

Vince seems to have a very close relationship with his daughter, Lauren. When I ask Vince about it, he says, "I actually was never that close to Lauren when she was a young child." He then proceeds to tell me a story of how a horse, Zing, brought Lauren and him closer and allowed him to discover what a wonderful daughter he has. That is Zing's gift.

This story is written in Vince's voice as he tells it to me, but I also interject Zing's thoughts from time to time. "How is that possible?" you ask. Well, as mentioned in "Shakespeare's Own Tale," Vince and Lauren use to take me out to the stable when Lauren went riding. What I failed to mention is that while they were busy, I closely observed the horses and listened to their neighing. Horses are actually quite straight forward creatures, and their language reflects that. Also, you can tell a lot about what horses are thinking by watching their ears. They use their ears much like humans use their hands. When their ears point toward you, they are giving you their full attention. When their ears are straight back, watch out! Anyway, after learning the intricacies of the English and Cat languages, Horse was relatively easy.

Vince: *I wasn't too surprised when I found out that Shakespeare could speak Horse. His ability at languages seems to know no bounds.*

Shakespeare: *Anyway, my second tale opens in a car with Vince and Lauren going out to a stable for the first time.*

Chapter One: Lauren Finds Zing

Who is my daughter?
Sadly, I am too busy,
But Zing brings us close.

"I CAN'T BELIEVE IT'S REAL. We're actually going. You're taking me riding," says my youngest daughter, fourteen-year-old Lauren.

She has the biggest grin and look of anticipation on her face that I've ever seen.

"You've been such a good kid, your mom and I want to fulfill this wish of yours," I reply.

As strange as it may seem, I really didn't know Lauren very well. We'd never formed a father-daughter bond. As an assistant professor in microbiology, I was always busy in the laboratory, supervising my students or doing my own research. It had fallen, unfairly, to my wife, Alice, to do most of the child-rearing. The little that I did know about Lauren had been learned, largely, from what others told me rather than by personal observation or in conversations with her.

Her preschool teacher, Mrs. Mills told me, "Lauren clung onto me for the whole first week of preschool; I had a third leg!"

However, preschool did help Lauren, since her teacher later told me that she was gradually coming out of her shell. I also learned from Mrs. Mills of a remarkable trait that Lauren still possesses and proves to be invaluable in her horseback riding – an ability to focus and concentrate. As part of a school assignment, she made pin pricks on a world map, to outline the continents. Although she was only four, she worked away at that project for over three hours straight. I have a hard time focusing on something for more than an hour without taking a break!

Also, through a story my dad told me, I learned that she is very diligent and always wants to see that things are carried out correctly; a trait she again uses in her equestrian efforts. Thus, when Dad and my mom were babysitting Lauren one time, my dad was watching a football game that was crucial to him. In the presence of Lauren, my mom told Dad to be sure to mow the lawn while she went out to run some errands. Mom had not been gone ten minutes when Lauren pulled on Dad's sleeve and reminded him,

"Grandpa, Grandma said you should mow the lawn."

My dad replies, "In a little while dear. I'm watching my game now."

"But Grandpa, you are supposed to mow the lawn now."

This back and forth went on for a while, until Dad finally got up and mowed the lawn. He had decided that he could do it now, or do it later, but Lauren was not going to give him any peace until the lawn was mowed like Grandma said. He never did get to see the end of the game, since this was before you could tape TV programs.

As informative as these stories are, I now decide it is time I make room in my life for my youngest daughter, and perhaps horseback riding will create a link between us.

As we pull into the stable grounds, Lauren's anticipation is palpable. We are greeted by a teenager.

"Hi. You must be Lauren. I'm Paula. I'll be teaching you today on Zing."

"That's a catchy name," I reply.

"Her real name is Quite Amazing, but everyone just calls her by her barn name, Zing. Anyway, Lauren, first you have to get her groomed. Grace will help you prepare her for your ride."

Now Grace doesn't look like she is more than seven or eight years old. I'm skeptical that someone so young can do the job, but I need not have feared.

"Come inside the stable, and we can get Zing ready," motions Grace as she starts toward an opening in the barn.

Inside is far from a grand affair. As soon as we enter, we smell the stench of horse manure, which *perfumes* the air. Flies are our constant companions and keep the horses' tails busy swishing them away. Cobwebs decorate the rafters in the ceiling, and the wooden stalls have chew marks from years of horses whiling away the hours while waiting for the next time they will be ridden. If it wasn't for Lauren's enthusiasm for riding, I would have left immediately. In each stall, a hay net hangs next to a water bucket; the horses attack these nets with vigor as they munch away. Between the hay, dust and horse hair, this is an asthma sufferer's worst nightmare, which is one reason our older daughter, Laurel, never goes to a stable. Grace leads us to a stall with Zing's name on it.

"I'll get Zing and then show you how to groom her," says Grace as she opens Zing's door.

After leading her out of her stall, Grace hooks up her halter[1] to two straps that are fastened to both sides of the aisle.

---

[1] Headgear that fits behind a horse's ears and around its muzzle.

"You pick the dirt and manure out of the "V" in the bottom of her hooves like this," instructs Grace as she wields a wooden object with a pointed metal pick jutting out from it, which she calls a hoof pick. "We now have to brush your horse," Grace says as she demonstrates the proper technique.

Each brush has its own purpose. It's quite overwhelming, but Grace has it all mastered. Next, we put on the saddle and reins after wiping the dust from them. Both are old and worn; they show years of use without proper cleaning.

Grace warns us, "Horses are real tricksters. Before you put on the saddle, they bloat out their bellies, so when you cinch up the strap that holds on the saddle, called a girth, it won't be tight after they exhale. When a greenhorn tries to get on, the saddle slips, and the rider ends up falling on their butt. All the horses then get a good laugh. So, after you put on the saddle you have to cinch up the girth again just before you get on, when you can catch the horse off guard."

We next lead Zing out to the corral where Paula is waiting for us.

"Okay Lauren, you always get on a horse from its left side," Paula instructs.

She then attaches a long piece of rope to Zing and off they go at a walk on a circle. Lauren is just beaming; she is so happy.

"Push the horse forward with your seat, Lauren. That's it... You know, Lauren is a natural," Paula says, nodding to me. "Okay, Lauren, we're going to try the trot[2] now. Just gently squeeze your lower legs together and push more with your seat and lower back."

"I'm trying, but she won't trot," says Lauren with a dismal look on her face.

"That's okay", says Paula, "It will take time for you to build up those muscles."

---

[2] A two-beat gate with diagonal legs moving in synchrony.

Paula makes a clicking sound with her mouth and gives Zing a little tap on her rump with a whip. Zing then starts to trot.

"Let the movement of Zing lift your seat out of the saddle. That's it. That will keep you from bouncing so much. That's called posting."

Although Lauren looks a little afraid for a while, eventually she relaxes and starts to grin again. Paula brings Zing down to a walk to cool her off, and the lesson is over.

I ask Paula, "What kind of horse is Zing?"

"She's a chestnut mare, quarter horse, thoroughbred cross with a little bit of Arab. That's a perfect mixture for an all-around horse," Paula replies as she pats Zing's neck.

Lauren and I take Zing into the barn and remove her reins, put on her halter, and then hook her up to the side straps attached to posts in the aisle. We then have a chance to talk.

While I take off Zing's saddle, I ask Lauren, "When did you decide you wanted to ride horses?"

As Lauren starts to brush Zing she says, "I've always just loved animals, and when I was little you bought me a rocking horse with springs. I just loved the motion of that horse; it felt like flying. But then you got rid of it."

"It was so bulky, we didn't want to have to pay for it when we moved. Also, we thought you'd out-grown it."

"Well I hadn't. I was sad when it wasn't at our new house."

"I'm sorry honey."

"That's okay Daddy, at least I get to ride a real horse now."

Lauren has never been a demonstrative child when it comes to her emotions, but on the way home, she puts her head on my shoulder and whispers, "Thank you Daddy for taking me riding."

On Paula's recommendation, we make our first of many trips to a tack store.[3] She advised Lauren to get a pair of riding pants and her own fitted helmet. We also buy Lauren a pair of relatively inexpensive boots, though none of this equipment is cheap. In subsequent lessons, Lauren becomes better at posting and doesn't bounce so much. It looks easy, so I decide to take a few lessons. It means another trip to the tack store and more money spent. This definitely is not a sport for the frugal.

When I try posting, I always get it wrong. You're supposed to know when to lift yourself out of the saddle by watching the horse's shoulder, but when I think it's time to start up, it's too late. So finally I decide to rise up out of the saddle when I think it's the wrong time and sure enough I end up doing it correctly. Lauren is infinitely better at posting. We then take up cantering.[4] The thing about cantering is it goes really fast. Everything you pass is just a blur. Now the natural impulse is to grip the horse with your thighs. The only trouble is that this action signals the horse to go faster. The faster the horse goes, the tighter you squeeze. Generally, this scenario does not end well, since it usually continues until the rider falls off. The correct posture is to relax your thighs and tighten your calf muscles. This may sound easy, but you have no idea how hard this is until you try it. To complicate matters even more, the horse has to lead with its inside leg. I inevitably have the horse on the wrong lead. Again, Lauren is much more adept at this than I am.

The next step is jumping. I can just hear people asking, "Whatever possesses this old guy to want to leave the ground when on a horse? Is he crazy?" Well, I probably am, but my reasoning is, *If we go out on a trail ride and the horse decides it wants to jump over*

---

[3] A store selling riding equipment, also called a saddle shop.

[4] A three-beat gate with the inside leg leading. The outside leg leads in a counter canter.

something, I should be ready. The only thing scarier than cantering is jumping. As the horse just starts to jump, you are supposed to come up out of the saddle and off the horse's back; however, when you do this, you see this enormous head coming up right at your face. If you do it right, the horse's head does not smack you right between the eyes. Needless to say, the first time I didn't do it right. It's hard to explain how a horse gave you a black eye! As usual, while I failed my first time, Lauren succeeded beautifully. I finally get the hang of it, sort of, and do really enjoy going on trail rides. I even manage to hang on while my horse jumps over a bush. But I finally come to my senses and decide to *hang up my spurs* while I am still in one piece. I also feel it's wise to spend our limited horse budget on the obvious talent of my daughter, Lauren.

As Lauren's riding skill continues to improve, her instructor says she feels Lauren is ready to enter one of the stable's little local horse shows. We are flattered, so off we go again to the tack store to get Lauren a show jacket, a modest and more or less inexpensive one, which again is not the same as cheap! I fully understand when I hear that one father offers his daughter the most expensive tennis racket in the world if she will only give up riding. But riding makes Lauren so happy, and I do still owe her for getting rid of her childhood bouncy horse.

On the day of the competition, Lauren admonishes me, "Hurry up Daddy, I don't want to be late for the show."

I blithely reply, "That's okay Lauren. I'm sure we have lots of time."

Well, we did not. This is the one time that the roads are crowded on a Sunday morning due to construction. By the time we arrive at the stable, all the *easy-to-ride* horses are already taken. So Lauren has to settle for Ralph, who is notorious for being lazy. Lauren also must use the oldest and most ratty saddle and reins. We finally get Ralph ready, and Lauren just makes it into the ring in time for her first class[5], which is riding on the flat. I take my seat next to some seasoned riders who are waiting for their classes to start. I can't help but notice that they are wearing more expensive looking riding jackets than Lauren. Their confident manner is unsettling. The class begins with the walk and then proceeds onto the trot. I lean over to one of the experienced riders on the bench and brag,

"That's my daughter, the one in the brown tweed jacket. She looks pretty good, doesn't she?"

"Her posting is off," is the curt response.

When it's time for the canter, Lauren's horse just won't canter at first, but with persistence, Lauren finally persuades Ralph."

"There, she did it. Her canter looks pretty good," I try to float another compliment for Lauren.

"She's on the wrong lead," is the terse reply from my seat mate.

Lauren's next class is jumping over barriers that my bench companions inform me are two thirds of a meter high[6]. I feel quite a bit more confident since Lauren can easily clear these jumps during her lessons, but that is on Zing. Using all her skill, Lauren manages to get Ralph cantering on the correct lead and over the first jump successfully. I find myself leaping up off my bench with each jump that Lauren faces. She is having the ride of her life, but then Ralph's laziness catches up with them. With two jumps left to go, Ralph figures he's done for the day and refuses to do any more. I'm heartbroken, especially since Lauren's poor showing is my fault for not listening to her and leaving the house too late. Needless to say, there are no ribbons for Lauren. As we lead Ralph into the aisle for grooming before we put him away, I apologize to Lauren,

"I'm sorry honey. I let you down. We should have left earlier."

---

[5] One of the judged rides in a riding competition.

[6] One meter is 3.3 feet.

Lauren replies, "That's okay Daddy. It's fun showing, and Christina (the girl who won the classes) really wants to win."

I give Lauren a big hug out of gratitude and love for letting me off the hook like that. Riding has thus let me discover the warmth and maturity that my daughter possesses. I also have learned how conscientious and diligent she is. While most kids might give up after such a disastrous show, Lauren works even harder on all the gaits. She also practices on all different horses, even Ralph, so she can master her signals to the horse. When it comes time for the second show, I have learned my lesson. We are one of the first people to arrive. Lauren has her pick of equipment and, most importantly, she can ride Zing. This time she places third in her flat class and second in her jumping class. On the way home I commend Lauren,

"I'm proud of you honey. You did so well."

"I'm glad you're happy Daddy. You're the best for taking me riding. I just want to make you proud, and I really love to be around horses."

In the next show, even though Lauren could still enter the beginner classes because she has not yet won a class, she decides to enter the more advanced classes with Christina and the other seasoned riders. She feels that is only fair. We both know that she will probably not win any ribbons. I'm scheduled to take part in our church service, so I just drop her off at the stable. After church, I go to pick up Lauren. As I pull up to the stable parking lot, Lauren comes running over to the car.

"Daddy, I won both of my classes. Zing was so good."

She has the biggest grin on her face and holds up two first-place ribbons. We all go out to dinner to celebrate.

"I'm so happy with Zing. She did great," says Lauren.

"I'm sure you have a lot to do with it," I reply.

"I couldn't have done it without Zing," insists Lauren in all modesty.

I thus learn how exceptional Lauren really is. While many kids would have been crowing about how great they are, Lauren can only praise her horse. In subsequent shows, Lauren is generally in the ribbons, usually first. I overhear one of the competitors say,

"Is that Lauren girl coming to the next show? She always wins!"

It comes down to the last show to determine who will win the trophy for the best performance for all the shows. It's between Christina and Lauren. All the parents are there, including Christina's. They have just bought Christina her favorite horse from the stable, so she can ride him in all the classes. Lauren rides Zing again. Lauren wins the flat class, and Christina is second. Lauren and Christina now are tied. It will all come down to the final jumping class. Christina and her horse look unbeatable. They easily clear all the fences, but the last one. On this jump, her horse's toe just ticks the rail.[7] It teeters in its cup, and then it falls. A big "Ohhh" rises up from the crowd. Then it's Lauren's turn. As she and Zing approach each jump, I lunge forward as if I can lift Lauren and Zing over each jump by sheer willpower. Then she comes to the last jump. Like Christina's horse, Zing's toe nicks the rail. Again the pole rocks in the cup, back and forth, back and forth. I can't breathe. Then it settles back into its holder! Lauren wins the class and the trophy. Ecstasy! I can't contain myself as I jump up and down and cheer at the top of my lungs. It's thrilling when Lauren receives her trophy. Afterwards Lauren seems a little concerned.

"What's the matter honey? You won!"

"I know, but Christina and her family look so sad."

---

[7] The pole over which a horse jumps.

I turn in their direction, and sure enough, they appear quite glum. I thus learn that Lauren is more sensitive towards the feelings of others than me.

Shakespeare: *Here Vince chokes up a bit with emotion. I think his memories of how he and Lauren formed such a close bond gets to him. While he retires into the kitchen for a drink, I have a chance to consult my notes from my conversations with Zing on how she feels about what happens next in this tale. She's a little shy, but friendly. Zing tells me that she is very sad when her favorite girl, who she calls Apples because she brings these tasty delights, stops coming to ride her. She always feels like a machine when the other kids ride her. They just slap on the saddle; sometimes they don't even pick out the mud and stones from her feet. The pebbles then hurt her hooves. No one loves her the same way Apples does, but Zing is quite stoic and does her job no matter how she feels. Then one day, she is led out of her stall and into a big box with round things that roll.*

Zing relays her concerns at the time. "Where are they taking me? What's going to happen to me?"

About this time Vince comes back, so I put my notes away. Vince looks refreshed as he sits down and continues his story.

Chapter Two: A New Home

ABOUT THIS TIME, LAUREN and I view a horse movie that takes place in a magnificent stable. The entrance way has a beautiful stone wall. Inside, the stalls are all large and well maintained. The rafters lack cobweb curtains. The arena, where the horses are ridden, even has a chandelier. The riders are performing maneuvers that we have never seen before. It is all so exciting that it overwhelms us. Both Lauren and I decide that she has learned as much as she can at her current stable, and it is time to move on. We hear of a new place that is supposed to be good, called Old Mill Stable, so we decide to give it a try.

As we pull into the stable grounds, both our mouths fall open in amazement. There is a beautiful stone entrance way into the stable just like we saw in the movie! At the entrance, we are greeted by a lady who introduces herself as Mary and then proceeds to show us around. In contrast to our previous stable, the stalls are large and filled with straw instead of sawdust, so they are less dusty for the horses and us humans. The barn is free from manure with its incumbent odor, and the fly population is reduced to the occasional intruder. Instead of water buckets, there is an automatic system that provides fresh water whenever the horses want it. The saddles and reins are all clean and well maintained. But the best thing is the excellent footing for the horses – both in the inside arena and outside ring. The only thing it lacks is the chandelier! Mary explains that Lauren will be learning to ride dressage on Zing. When I ask Mary about Zing, she explains that Old Mill Stable has just bought Zing as a schooling horse. Lauren is delighted to see her old friend again.

As Lauren gets Zing ready for her lesson, I ask, "What's dressage?"

Mary explains, "Horses are naturally balanced until a rider gets on their back; then the weight gets shifted onto its front legs, and the horse is unbalanced and loses control. Dressage teaches the rider to use their back muscles to sit into the horse, which shifts the weight back onto the horse's hind legs, so the horse and rider become balanced."

"That sounds easy enough," I naïvely say.

"It may sound easy, but it's the kind of thing you strive for your whole life," Mary assures me. "I'm still working on it myself."

Lauren's first dressage lesson is on a lunge line[8]. I can see Lauren starting to use her back muscles to balance the horse in response to Mary's urging. However, it's obvious this process is going to be a long one. After the lesson, I ask Lauren, "How was it?"

---

[8] A line attached to the horses bridle so the horse goes in a circle. This arrangement allows the rider to work on position and other aspects of riding without having to worry about steering.

"I'm beginning to have more control, but my back muscles are a little sore", she replies.

After a few dressage lessons, Lauren has her first jumping lesson at this new stable.

Lauren observes, "I can really feel how much more control dressage gives me, and Zing is so good. It's like she knows where to take off for her jump."

After her lesson, Lauren takes off Zing's saddle and starts to brush her. Zing reaches back with her head and pokes Lauren with her nose.

"I love when she does that. She's reminding me that her lesson is over, and it's time for her treat," says Lauren as she takes a mint out of her pocket and gives it to Zing.

Lauren leads Zing into her stall and watches as she begins to attack her hay. Since the other horses are beginning to be fed, Lauren brings Zing's feed to her, which she eats with vigor. Afterwards, Zing nuzzles Lauren while Lauren gives her a hug. A real bond of love and respect is beginning to develop between the two of them.

A month after we arrived at Old Mill Stable, we get the news. The stable has received many offers to buy Zing, so they decide to sell her. Knowing how close Lauren and Zing have become, they offer her to us first. If we refuse, Zing will go to a buyer from outside the stable. There is no doubt that Zing's the right horse for Lauren at her stage of riding development. The question is, can we afford not only Zing, but all the expenses that go with owning her – the board fees, the saddle, reins, plus the cost of lessons? Alice and I talk it over while Lauren holds her breath. Lauren never says anything, but we know she will be heartbroken if she loses Zing. We finally decide that we can refinance our mortgage and manage it. Money will be tight for a while, but we feel the look of pure joy on Lauren's face makes buying Zing very worthwhile.

"Oh Mommy, Daddy, I can't believe it. Thank you, thank you, thank you," and she hugs us both as tight as she can. "Can we go out right now and buy Zing? Can we?"

"Well, the bank has already been called and all the arrangements made, so I guess we can." Is my reply.

With that, Lauren races out to the car and waits for Alice and me.

"Can we stop at the store and get some carrots and apples to give Zing?" Lauren asks.

"Sure honey, why not?" I reply.

After we arrive at the stable, I write the check, and Lauren rushes out to the stalls.

I go to Zing's stall just in time to hear Lauren exclaim "You're going to be my horse forever and forever."

She then takes Zing out for a walking hack[9] and spends all afternoon with her. She grooms her and feeds her apples and carrots while Zing keeps nuzzling her. It is a real love affair. After we buy Zing, Lauren starts riding her every Monday through Saturday, and on Sunday she goes out to visit her, giving her lots of carrots and apples. The other riders at the stable become her best human friends. Her whole world is centered on Zing and her riding. The combination of Lauren's ability to focus and concentrate and Zing's jumping ability allows them to become excellent at going over obstacles. Zing can even jump meter[10] verticals[11] and oxers.[12] It is now time for Lauren and Zing to enter their first jumping competition held at Old Mill Stable. The first and second riders in Lauren's class each knock off two rails. Then it's Lauren's turn. As

[9] An outdoor ride just for fun.

[10] A meter is approximately 39 inches.

[11] A vertical jump with the width of only a pole.

[12] Two vertical jumps placed together to give the jump width as well as height.

she and Zing clear the jumps, my body is taking each jump with them. Their round is clear until Lauren relaxes just a hair at the last jump. Zing catches a toe on the rail, and it comes down. Two of the subsequent competitors go clear with no rails down; thus, Lauren and Zing finish third.

As we put Zing away in her stall, Lauren says, "It's my fault Daddy, I quit before the last jump."

"I know honey, but knowing that you can't stop until your task is finished is an important lesson to learn for both riding and life," I say as I hug her. Lauren nods in agreement.

Lauren continues to improve at jumping schooling shows. She and Zing start to win most of the classes they enter. They do so well that Mary suggests they enter a Province-wide recognized jumping show. Pulling into the show grounds, we can see the outstanding quality of the competition horses.

"These are the best of the best," I declare to Lauren.

"I don't care. Zing can beat all of them," Lauren replies.

When we looked over the course, many jumps contain a picket-fence-like gate leaning at an angle. I ask one of the spectators about these jumps.

"Oh, these are sloping gate jumps," he replies. "They're quite common at these competitions."

These jumps are indeed common. Zing and Lauren have never seen such a jump, so I'm not sure how they will respond.

"Zing can do it," is Lauren's terse comment.

When it's Lauren's and Zing's turn, Zing canters into the ring and easily takes all the jumps until she comes to the first sloping gate jump. Zing's eyes open wide in fear, and her ears go straight back. She veers away in refusal. Lauren brings her around again and on the third attempt manages to get her over the jump. This scenario is repeated at each sloping gate jump. I can see Lauren's frustration level building, but at the last sloping gate jump, Lauren manages to get Zing over the jump on the first try. As Lauren and Zing leave the ring, Lauren is almost in tears while the judge yawns in boredom.

"That's okay dear," I say. "The important thing is that you did not quit. I've never been more proud of you."

"And of Zing," Lauren adds.

In the subsequent days, Mary has Lauren and Zing work on sloping gates until Zing can go over them without hesitation. Consistent with Mary's training methods, Lauren and Zing start with a half meter jump and then steadily increased the height until Zing can clear a meter sloping gate without refusing.

Early one morning, I drive Lauren to the stable. She has volunteered to help give the horses their morning feed and clean out their stalls. She just loves being around the horses. As we make our way up to the stable, Gustave, the German professional for the stable, is riding a magnificent tawny brown horse. They are undulating up and down in a trot on the spot. Both Lauren and I watch in amazement as we observe the horse's muscles flexing and relaxing to a rhythmic, relentless silent beat. The horse's neck is arched, and as the rising sun hits the vapor rising from the horse's body, both horse and rider seemed to be engulfed in a golden glow. "Who is that horse?" I ask a fellow observer.

"Oh, that's Skotch," she says. "He's a Westphalian[13] gelding from Germany. Gustave's getting him ready for his next dressage competition."

Even after Lauren goes into the stable to take care of the horses, I can't take my eyes off this magnificent animal!

Lauren continues to progress in her riding. I notice that every time Lauren rides on the flat, Alana, Gustave's wife and an excellent dressage rider in her own right, watches intently. One day

[13] A horse with origins in Westphalia in Germany.

when it's time for Lauren's dressage lesson, Alana comes out instead of Mary.

"I'll be teaching Lauren dressage from now on. Mary will continue teaching her jumping. Is that okay?"

I nod in agreement. While Mary is a good overall rider, her specialty is jumping. I conjecture that Alana sees great promise in Lauren and has convinced Mary to let her take over Lauren's dressage lessons. Alana's added skill and experience is apparent with her first lesson. Under Alana's tutelage, Lauren and Zing really began to develop the muscles necessary for Zing to carry her weight on her hind end. These lessons, in turn, greatly improve Zing's jumping ability. Lauren and Zing can now easily go over combination jumps[14] a meter high. With this added ability, they start to often win jumping classes for advanced riders at other stables in addition to those at Old Mill Stable. Lauren and Zing also made great strides in their dressage training. They pass a real milestone when they win a basic dressage class at a Province wide recognized show. This victory is particularly significant since Zing does not have the build for a dressage horse, so Lauren and Zing must depend on the skill they've learned from Alana.

Shakespeare: *Towards the end of Vince's narrative I notice he is yawning a lot. Sensing he is getting tired, I suggest that we call it a night, so he can feed me and take me out for my evening walk. After we finish, Vince goes up to bed. Before I retire for the night, I check my notes to get Zing's feelings about what we have covered in this chapter.*

"What I really love to do is jump." Those words sum up Zing's sentiment. She also says. "I find riding on the flat rather boring and hard. Apples keeps making me bend and lengthen and shorten my stride. My

[14] Several jumps in a row set a certain number of strides apart.

muscles are quite tired when she finishes. I just wish we could gallop in the open spaces and go over jumps.

The next day when I ask Vince about this passion of Zing's, he says, "Just wait till the next part of her story. You'll see her fondest dream comes true."

Chapter Three: Galloping Free

AFTER THEIR LESSON, LAUREN always takes Zing on a walking hack to cool off. On one such occasion, a group of riders gallops by them. One thing we find out about Zing that day is that she can't stand to be beaten in a race. Zing takes off at a gallop. I can see Zing lower her body as her stride increases, and she forges into the lead. Lauren is not use to galloping in the open, but fortunately her riding skill allows her to hang on. Riders standing next to me start to yell, "Circle! Circle!" I don't think Lauren can hear their yells, but, using her instincts, she finally starts to take this action, and Zing reluctantly stops.

After this experience, we both feel it's time for Lauren to learn to ride cross-country. It so happens that Lauren and I receive a book as a present on how to ride cross-country from a friend who knows of Lauren's and my interest in horses. In essence, it instructs the rider to start by learning how to position their weight when walking the horse up and down a hill. Using the same principle, we then work up to trot and gallop. The hardest situation is riding along the side of a hill because the horse's left and right legs are on two different levels. Lauren and Zing master these skills rather quickly. I find that the same method I use in the classroom also applies here. Start simple and then build up in a gradual manner. Lauren and I work together on cross-country riding, which makes the bond between us even stronger than it was before. After learning to ride in the open, Lauren and Zing then progress to taking cross-country jumps. For this step, we enlist Mary's help.

As Mary explains, "What's hard about a cross-country jump is that you are taking it at a gallop. Therefore, you must be able to gather your horse enough to enable them to take the jump without breaking the stride of the horse."

Mary instructs, "Okay Lauren, you and Zing start by taking this portable jump on the flat at the gallop. We will start with these jumps since they fall down if hit; regular cross-country jumps are nailed in place and are immovable. Thus, if you hit them, they don't give, you do, much to your regret."

The first time, Zing hits her hoof on the rail; fortunately, this is not a cross-country jump, so it topples. The second time, Lauren gathers Zing enough, so they clear the jump quite easily. After a few times, Zing can take the jump at a gallop in one continuous flowing movement. Watching this is a real thing of grace and beauty. I next help Mary drag the jump components part way up a hill. This is quite an arduous chore since the jumps are heavier than they look! Jumps on an incline pose the problem of making the horse carry enough momentum up a slope to be able to take the jump. With coaching from Mary, Lauren and Zing master this obstacle without much trouble because, although Zing is not a very big horse, she can generate a lot of power from her hind end.

Finally, I help Mary lug and set up jumps at both the top and bottom of a hill, so Lauren and Zing can jump them going downhill. Mary explains, "This combination of jumps is the most difficult because, after taking the first jump, you have to collect Zing enough to take the bottom jump." I would never even try this terrifying prospect, but Lauren is determined. As she takes the first jump and careens down the hill, right towards the jump at the bottom, I can hardly watch. I'm sure she and Zing are going to smash right into it. I can see Lauren fighting to bring Zing under control. Just as it looks like disaster, Lauren manages to gather Zing, and they sail over the jump. I gasp in relief. Against my strong protest, Lauren insists on repeating the operation. Again, I can barely look as she clears the first jump, but this time she's able to control Zing much better and takes the bottom jump with ease.

As Lauren is walking Zing back to the barn I exclaim, "I'm so proud of you Lauren. You're wonderful, but you and Zing about gave me a heart attack."

"It's Zing you should be proud of," replies Lauren. "She's unbelievable. I see now why they named her Quite Amazing. I just love her so much. I'm going to spend all afternoon with her, grooming her, grazing her, and giving her lots of apples and carrots!"

Lauren is as good as her word, and her response shows me a characteristic that is rare in people. No matter how much I try to praise Lauren for her riding, she always defers the praise to Zing. She doesn't have an arrogant bone in her body. I have Zing to thank for helping me appreciate what a rare and wonderful daughter Lauren is.

The next cross-country lesson involves water jumps. Just like people and dogs, some horses like water and some do not. Fortunately, Zing does not seem to mind water at all. Whether it is jumps into or out of the water, Zing takes it all in her stride (literally). In fact, Lauren uses Zing to help riders with horses that are not enthusiastic about water. Lauren and Zing first enter the water and the other horses, being herd animals, will dip their toes and eventually follow. When I comment to Laura that she may have to compete against these same horses in the future, she says she only hopes she has been able to assist them. Finally, Mary decides that Lauren and Zing are ready to try the fixed cross-country jumps. They don't seem to have much trouble with these jumps.

Even the in and out jump[15] does not pose a problem. But then she's faced with the dreaded picnic table jump. This jump looks like its namesake – it's a meter high and just over a meter wide. Like all the cross-country jumps, it's as solid as steel.

"You don't have to try this one," I say, hoping she'll agree.

At first Lauren hesitates, but then her stubbornness wins out and she replies, "Zing and I can do it!"

She takes Zing back about ten meters and starts to gallop toward the jump. I half hide my eyes in fear. Just about two meters in front of the jump Zing veers away. I breathed a sigh of relief.

"Okay that's enough for today," I demand with as much determination as I can muster.

"No Dad, we can't leave it with a refusal," Lauren says in an emphatic voice.

"I know we don't usually like to quit with a refusal, but maybe we should call it a day," offers Mary.

"No! Zing and I can do this," declares Lauren. With that she takes Zing back a longer distance than before and gives her a pat. I hear her exclaim with a loud and determined voice, "Come on girl. Let's show them!" So off they go. This time I really can't watch. I cover my eyes and pray – actions that would be repeated a lot when Lauren rides cross-country. I remove a few fingers from my eyes just in time to see Lauren and Zing clearing the jump.

"See, I told you Zing could do it," declares Lauren triumphantly.

After silently thanking The Almighty, I gasp, "Thank God you are alright."

"You know, very few horses have ever cleared this jump, and they were all much bigger than Zing," exclaims Mary in amazement.

---

[15] A jump in the form of a square with a set number of strides between the two opposite sides.

"Yes, but they didn't have Zing's heart," declares Lauren.

I then begin to realize what a rare horse we have, but even more, how brave and persistent Lauren can be if she believes in something.

In light of Zing's and Lauren's success, Mary has Lauren sign up to enter a cross-country meet. As we arrive at the competition grounds, the first thing I see is an ambulance that's parked, just waiting for disaster. This sight does nothing to relieve my apprehension. Lauren is so excited; I'm petrified. At these types of meets, the horses don't get to see the jumps before-hand; however, the riders and their supporters can walk the course and plan how to take all the jumps. One jump that particularly catches my eye is an open pit that is a meter wide. Lauren and Zing have never seen such a jump. The jump is particularly difficult because it's partially grown over with brush. Lauren will have to tell Zing where to jump. If Lauren and Zing miss the jump, Lauren can end up in the pit with Zing on top of her.

"I don't think you and Zing should do this jump. Zing has no experience with it. Remember a rider was killed earlier in the year trying to jump a similar jump," I tell Lauren.

"Yes, but he wasn't riding Zing," she replies.

"I still don't think it's a good..."

"No! Zing and I can do this." With that Lauren stomps off.

I start after her, but Mary intervenes.

"I'm sure she and Zing can do it. My experience with kids is that there are times when you have to trust them."

I'm still reluctant, but I decide to let her go ahead with the competition. The riders take the course singly and are timed. Lauren is the tenth rider to go. As the whistle blows, she and Zing gallop off. The first part of the course goes according to plan. Zing's ability to take jumps smoothly without breaking her stride lives up to her name, Quite Amazing. As the dreaded open pit jump looms ahead, I start to pray that God will protect them. Half hiding my eyes, the Higher Powers must have heard because Lauren gives Zing the signal to jump at just the right time. They sail over the trench and motor on out of sight behind some trees. The next jumps I can see are by the finish line. The rider's horse must jump a meter fence, into a paddock, make a quick turn without retracing its steps, which would count as a refusal, and then immediately jump a second one meter jump out of the paddock before crossing the finish line. I hardly dare breathe, waiting for Lauren and Zing to emerge from the trees.

"There they are," I can't help but yell, though I'm sure no one is listening to me. Lauren and Zing easily take the first fence.

"Don't retrace your path," I yell. But Lauren and Zing are way ahead of me. They made a perfect turn and jump out of the paddock, and then gallop across the finish line. As I run up to them, I'm thanking The Lord for delivering them safely.

"Thank goodness you're okay."

"I told you we could do it. Zing was so wonderful. She didn't miss a single jump."

A little later Mary comes running up, "You and Zing have the fastest time of the day with no jumping penalties. You won the competition. You and Zing even beat last year's champion!"

After we return to the stable, Lauren gives Zing lots of carrots and apples as she brushes her. She then puts the first-place ribbon on Zing's stall.

"Zing's the one that really earned this ribbon," Lauren says, deflecting the praise to Zing as is her habit. Alice and I then take Lauren, Mary and Laurel out for a celebratory dinner at Lauren's favorite restaurant.

Given Zing's all-around abilities in both dressage and jumping, Mary suggests that Lauren and Zing next enter a Province wide one-day event. This competition includes a morning dressage test and an afternoon cross-country and stadium jumping course. The riders' performance results in a certain number of penalty points for each part; the horse-rider combination with the lowest number of penalty points at the end is the winner. We've rented Zing a stall at the stable where the competition is being held, so she can rest between stages. We arrive first thing in the morning, get Zing settled, and then register. Looking down the list, there are more than fifty horses registered for the competition, including Paula from Lauren's first stable. The competition starts with the dressage test. Riders have the option to have the test read to them or to memorize it. Lauren memorizes her test, but I read it for her just in case she forgets something. After Lauren's test is over and we put Zing away in her stall, we're standing around the dressage ring. A rider walks by looking very distressed.

"What's wrong?" asks Lauren.

"My coach is supposed to read my test for me, but she hasn't arrived. I'm due to ride next, and I don't know what to do," the rider bursts out sobbing.

"Oh, that's okay. I'll read for you." Lauren offers.

"Oh, thank you so much. I don't know what I'd do otherwise," the rider gathers herself in relief.

After the dressage competition, Lauren and I check the standings. Lauren and Zing are in tenth place. Among those beating her are the Provincial champion who was pointed out to me by Mary and the woman whose test Lauren read. I comment on this fact, and Lauren only says she's happy she could help her and hopes that someone would do the same if she ever needs help.

It's now time to walk the cross-country course. In addition to the dreaded open pit jump, there's also an embankment jump. The horse and rider must jump up on the flat surface that's about a meter high, jump a barrier and then jump down off the other side of the embankment. This combination is difficult because the jumping efforts come in rapid succession and horses are generally not use to jumping up on and down from surfaces. The horse and rider also go over a jump that's in a pool of water. The water's only a few inches deep, but, if the horse hesitates at all, it can result in a fall or refusal. A fall means automatic elimination. Towards the end of the course, there's a jump at the beginning of a steep downhill path. At the bottom of the hill, the horse and rider are required to make a quick left turn around some trees and bushes, where they are suddenly faced with a meter jump. The jump's positioned so that the horse and rider will not see the jump until the last second, so the horse has to have full trust in the rider. Upon walking to the end of the course, I shudder because there is not only one, but two ambulances parked, just waiting.

A whistle signals the time for Lauren and Zing to start. They're off at a gallop as I watch through my binoculars, which I just bought for this occasion. They sail over an opening jump of half a meter, which is designed to get the horse off to a good start and ready for the harder jumps that are still to come. After several more jumps that pose no problems for Laura and Zing, the open pit jump looms. Taking advantage of their previous experience, Lauren and Zing clear this jump. When faced with the embankment, I can see Zing hesitate.

"No. A refusal will be disastrous," I shout aloud to no one in particular.

But thanks to Lauren's urging and Zing's courage, they're up on the bank, over the barrier and down. I run along the path, to bring the later jumps into view. By the time I spot Lauren and Zing again, they're approaching the water jump. Zing has been ridden into and out of water many times, but she has never had to clear a hurdle that's *in* the water. She bounds into the pond and splashes toward the obstacle. Will she refuse? Will she slip and plow into the jump despite the cleats we screw into her horseshoes? I needn't have feared. Zing easily clears the jump and on they gallop. Several more barriers later, Zing makes it over the jump at the top of the steep path. Zing and Lauren then disappear from view. I hold my breath and once again call on the Almighty.

"Oh please God, keep her safe! Don't let her fall and get hurt," I plead.

After what seems an eternity, they emerge at full gallop and sail over the final jump on the course. They made it! I run over to where Lauren is cooling out Zing.

"She did it! She did it! Zing was wonderful!" Lauren exclaims. "She cleared everything. She's so brave!"

"I saw you urge her on." I reply.

"No Daddy. It was all Zing," Lauren defers full credit to Zing as usual.

Zing was so fast, I was certain she had not incurred any time faults in addition to no jumping penalties. Upon checking the score board, this belief is confirmed. Quite a few riders have been eliminated, including Paula from Lauren's first stable. Others have incurred a lot of cross-country penalty faults. Lauren and Zing are now in third place. The Provincial champion and the rider whose test Lauren had read are the only ones ahead of her.

The last phase of the competition is stadium jumping. Again, the riders and coaches but not the horses can preview the course ahead of time to see the jumps. From my vantage point at the entrance gate, the jumps I particularly notice are an oxer over water; a three-jump combination with one stride in between jumps; and a skinny jump, only about a meter wide, which is half the width of other jumps. But the jump that makes me the most nervous is a sloping-gate jump. Zing has not seen such a jump for a while, and I'm not sure she'll remember. When Lauren and I go to get Zing out of the stall, she is not too eager.

"I know you're tired girl, but we only have one more course to jump," coaxes Lauren.

I think Zing only comes out because of Lauren, and she wouldn't have done it for anyone else. The riders compete in reverse order of their standings, so Lauren and Zing go before the two ahead of her. Zing manages all the jumps up to the skinny jump okay, but without quite the enthusiasm she had shown on the cross-country course. As Lauren discussed with Mary earlier, she takes the skinny jump head on even though she will sacrifice a few seconds.

"If you take the jump at an angle, it looks bigger to the horse than it is, and the horse might refuse," explains Mary.

After successfully taking the skinny jump, Zing and Lauren approach the sloping gate jump. I cover my eyes. When I look again, they're over the jump and the rail is still up! Zing remembered! They're at the last jump.

"Keep riding! Keep riding!" I yell. She's over the jump and has no jumping penalty faults. With Zing's speed, I also feel they have no time faults. As Lauren takes Zing back to her stall for a well-deserved rest, I watch the last two riders go.

The second-place rider also clears all the jumps up to the skinny jump. Will she take a chance and try the jump at an angle? No... just like Lauren, she takes it head on and clears it easily, but at the sloping gate jump, her horse veers sideways and refuses. No matter how the rider tries, the horse will not go over the sloping gate. She's eliminated from the competition. Even though that result puts Lauren in second place, I feel very sorry for this rider as she leaves the ring with her head bowed in defeat and in tears. I can't imagine how she feels after *all* she and her horse have gone through. It was going so well for her, and then this grueling competition ends in such a sudden misfortune. I feel like giving her a hug as she comes out of the ring, but she receives consolation from her coach and family.

The last to go is the Provincial champion. He looks quite confident of victory and a little arrogant. After all, he has been in this position many times before. He takes all the jumps up to the skinny jump with ease. I think, *he's taking the skinny jump at an angle! Will this be his demise?* No. His magnificent and undoubtedly very expensive horse clears the jump with little effort. As he approaches the sloping gate jump, my malicious side emerges and I chant quietly, "Miss it! Knock it down!" But unlike the previous rider, he clears it with no problem. I'm resolved to second place for Lauren and Zing. But as I started to turn away, his horse knocks down the last jump. He must have thought he'd won the competition and made the rookie mistake of relaxing and losing focus before the last jump. Lauren and Zing have won. They won!

Shakespeare: *At this point Vince lets out a laugh of joy, as he recalls this happy time. "It was such a long road for both of them; I'm just happy for their success," exclaims Vince. But then a cloud of sorrow comes over his face. "I almost forgot how this story ends," Vince declares with his head bowed.*

"Do you want to go on with it or should we just end the story here?" I ask.

Vince thinks a while and then replies, "No, Changing the story won't change how it really ends. I think we should tell the story the way it really happened, without any sugar coating." So Vince carries on:

Chapter Four: Triumph and Tragedy

THE RIBBONS ARE PRESENTED TO the riders mounted on their horses. When we go to get Zing out of her stall, she's more than reluctant.

"It's okay girl, you don't have to compete anymore. It's just so you can get your award," Lauren tries to explain to Zing.

It takes all of Lauren's persuasive powers and apples to get Zing out of her stall. Lauren then manages to mount Zing and walk her out to the award ceremony. Among all the cheers (mine are the loudest), Lauren and Zing receive their prizes. In addition to the first-place ribbon, they win a blanket with the words "Event Champion" on it. Seeing Lauren beaming, I know all our sacrifice has been worth it. When we arrive back at the stable, Lauren gives Zing an extra special grooming and lots of carrots and apples. As we leave, Zing looks quite content in her stall. Alice and I then treat Mary and our family to another grand feast at Lauren's favorite restaurant. It seems nothing can dampen our spirits.

Several days later we get the phone call all horse owners dread.

"Come to the stable quickly. I think your horse has colic.[16] We've already called the vet."

[16] An intestinal upset in horses that can be fatal.

Lauren and I race to the stable as fast as is possible without killing ourselves. As we run into the stable, we can hear Zing thrashing around and neighing out in pain in her stall. The vet's already there waiting for us. Zing's lying down sweating profusely and kicking at her belly, all classic signs of colic.

"You can save her, can't you?" pleads Lauren.

"Zing's in terrible pain. I have to put her down right now," answers the vet.

I have to hold Lauren back to keep her from rushing into the stall and getting kicked. I nod to the vet, and he gives Zing the fatal shot. Lauren falls into my arms; her body heaves with grief. In these circumstances, I'm usually quite a stoic person, but my eyes are wet with tears, which stream down my cheeks. As Zing lies still, Lauren brakes free from my grasp, runs into the stall and cradles Zing's head in her arms. There she quietly weeps.

"It's my fault. I shouldn't have given her all those apples and carrots. I should have been here to walk her," sobs Lauren.

"No! You're not to blame for this. It has nothing to do with you," I try to reassure her.

"The apples and carrots have nothing to do with this colic, and it wouldn't have mattered if you had been here or not. Chances are your horse's bowel got twisted. Believe me I've seen a lot of these, and you're not at all to blame," the vet said emphatically.

These words of reassurance do not abate Lauren's grief. I didn't realize how attached I've become to Zing. She has been so much more than just a wonderful, talented horse; she has changed our lives. Zing made me a better, more-caring man, but her greatest gift is allowing me to know and connect with Lauren and see what a truly wonderful daughter my wife and I have.

Zing Nuzzles Lauren

One of the last times Zing got to nuzzle Lauren

When I finally walk out of the stable with my arm around Lauren, I see two eyes watching us as we pass Skotch's stall. I suddenly have a premonition that Skotch's and Lauren's destiny will merge. It will save Lauren from total despair, and Zing will look down from Heaven and be glad.

Shakespeare: *It turns out that Vince's premonition does come true, and Lauren and Skotch compete very successfully in dressage. But that is a tale for another day.*

Tale Five: Tom Cat

Tom Cat
(Photo credit: Levent Konuk/Shutterstock)

Shakespeare: *When I come across a picture of Vince in his U.S. Air Force uniform, I get all excited. I reason he must have all kinds of daring combat exploits he can relate to me for our book. However, Vince dispels all my illusions when he tells me he was never in a war zone while in the service, but served in a military hospital in Ohio. However, Vince says that he did know a story from his military days that he thought I might use for the book; of course, we had to get permission and change the names. So, he tells me a story about Joe whom he met in the hospital. Joe had served in combat overseas and came home with PTSD. He eventually became homeless, and Vince lost track of him for quite a while. Then Vince got a letter from him saying he was all right, and a cat had saved him. Vince reads the letter to me, and Joe's story inspires me to write the following tale, which opens with Joe's nightmare.*

Chapter One: Joe's Nightmare

Bill's eyes haunted Joe.
Piercing eyes ruined his life,
But Tom Cat saved him.

"BILL! WATCH OUT! Sniper!" Joe yells.

Rat-tat-tat, the bullets fly everywhere.

"Oh God! I'm hit. Help me," screams Bill while writhing in agony.

"Bill, hang on I'm coming," Joe tries to reassure him.

Rat-tat-tat.

"That dam sniper. I can't reach Bill!" Joe mutters.

"Help me," Bill begs. "Oh, please Jesus. Mama help me. I can't stand it. Help!"

Every time Joe tries to reach out to Bill, that cursed sniper is waiting with his Rat-tat-tat. Joe knows the sniper's only keeping Bill alive to lure him out into the open. But he can't just leave Bill there. He can't stand Bill's screaming – that incessant howling! And those eyes. His eyes. Those pleading eyes staring at Joe. He can't take it anymore! "NO, NO, NOOOOOOOOOOOO!"

Joe is startled out of his restless sleep by the admonition, "Hey Joe. Wake up! You're having another one of those incessant nightmares."

Joe looks up, rubbing his eyes, and the blue uniform and face of Officer Grace comes into focus.

"I don't mind you sleeping on this hot air vent, but I'll have to run you off if you keep yelling like that. People will complain."

"Oh, sorry officer. I didn't mean to disturb anyone. It's just that..."

"Yeah I get it. I was in 'Nam also and know how bad it was. Say, why don't you sleep in one of the homeless shelters?"

"The beds are full of bedbugs and fleas. Besides, the dope addicts are always trying to steal my stuff. Anyway, it's time for me to start my rounds."

Joe rolls up his tattered blankets and puts them into his duffle bag. Before he goes to his begging spot, he stops by his kids' schoolyard and waits for them to play out in the yard before school starts. After about ten minutes, he spots them. Carrie is jumping rope and Mark is kicking a ball. He's careful that they don't see him. It breaks his heart not to be able to hold and kiss them, but he knows he can't in his state. Joe thinks, *They've grown so much since Martha left me. I know she had to, but it still torments me.*

After Joe's kids get called into school for their classes, Joe makes his way to the mall where people give him a wide berth. In particular, this is true for women with young children, which makes him very sad. He loves all children. Joe thinks, *How I miss my kids!* He takes out a worn, but loved picture of his family, or what used to be his family. He runs his fingers over their faces and kisses them. There is Martha. He doesn't blame her for divorcing him and taking the kids away. Joe knows that his erratic behavior and drinking were just too much for her. He realizes she tried, but she just couldn't take it anymore – if only he could get the image of Bill's pleading eyes out of his mind!

Joe goes into the public washroom and looks at himself in the mirror. He can see why people shun him. His hair is tangled, his face is haggard, his beard untidy, and his shirt looks like it hasn't been ironed in years. He takes out an old, brown bar of soap and washes his hands and face. As he looks again in the mirror, he sees Bill's eyes burrowing deep into his soul. He can't stand it.

"Make them go away," he screams as he smashes the mirror with his fists and runs, runs, runs! He doesn't stop until he reaches his spot on the heating grate. He lifts his bloody hands to his face and sobs incessantly.

The next day he takes his place on a street corner with his cap out. "Help a veteran. Just a little spare change," he pleads. When someone has pity on him and throws a few coins into his hat, he smiles in gratitude. After several hours, he accumulates enough to get a hamburger. As he squats on the sidewalk and starts to devour it, he spots a white cat staring at him, or more likely at his hamburger. As Joe looks at *him*, at least the cat struts around in a bold manner like Joe thinks of a *him*, he looks back suspiciously and starts to back away. Joe doesn't know why, but he throws a little piece of the hamburger out to him...

Vince: *I like your story so far, but what does the cat think of all this.*
Shakespeare: *Hey! Patience, patience. Do you want to tell this tale or shall I.*
Vince: *Okay. Sorry.*
Shakespeare: *Well, the cat's side of the story starts in a pound where he is patiently trying to get adopted.*

Chapter Two: A Stray Cat's Perils

WITH A CLANG, THE CAGE DOOR slams shut on a scruffy, white cat.

"Why'm I here. I ain't done nothin' wrong," he screeches to his cage in his own language,

"Let me outta this here stupid cell." He claws at the chain link fence that encloses him at the animal control center, but to no avail. He finally calms down and pouts as a stream of people parade in looking for feline pets, but all they want are kittens, certainly not an ill-tempered, bedraggled fireball. He laments to the walls of his cage,

"All people wanna git 're kittens. I've been stuck in this here prison forever. When them kittens start to play with their stupid ball that's in their cage, everyone 'Ohhs' and 'Ahhs' over them and just ignores me. They just wanna git to them kittens. There's nothin' I can do to compete with them. Don't those stupid people realize that they don't have ta wonder what I'll be like? What they see is what they git."

The cat finally decides, *If I ever wanna git outta here I'd better change my attitude.* However, no matter how cute this bedraggled cat tries to be, he just has no luck. As the last kitten gets adopted he thinks, *Yes! The last one's gone. Maybe now I can git outta here!* However, after several weeks the cat begins to lose hope. He starts to worry, *What happens if no one wants me? Will this place keep me forever or will they kill me and toss me out inta the alley?*

Then one day the stray cat sees a small, female human come down the aisle. She's young, but has a friendly face that looks to him like she'll be receptive if he pretends to be cute. He calls her Sweet Face because she has a smile that shines out love. His street sense has taught him how to read facial expressions. Sure enough, she comes over to him just as he turns on the charm and starts to play with a ball as a necessary evil. She pokes her finger into the cage, and he rubs against it and starts to purr. She then turns and talks to the attendant who shakes his head *No,* as he points at the cat with a frown on his face. The cat wonders, *Will she? Will I finally escape from here?* Despite the attendant's words of discouragement, Sweet Face persists, picks up the cat and carries him out of the pound. The cat inwardly exclaims, *Yes! Success!* They walk for what seems to Sweet Face's charge like forever, but finally she takes him into a house. She settles her new pet onto a nice soft cushion and feeds him. She then cuddles him, and he thinks, *Hey, this is great; maybe I'll stick around for a while.*

However, the feline's happiness is premature. When two adults come home, a tirade pierces the air. The women, whom he assumes is Sweet Face's mother, points at Sweet Face and her new friend and starts screaming. The cat decides to call her Meanie on the spot because of the permanent frown on her face. Sweet Face holds the cat tight and starts to cry. That doesn't stop the haranguing from Meanie. Finally, Sweet Face, with her pet clutched to her breast, runs upstairs into her bedroom and slams the door. She then blocks the door with her dresser. Meanie tries the door but can't open it. She keeps up her threatening thunder outside of Sweet Face's door for a while, but finally gives up. Sweet Face clutches her cat and snuggles with him on her bed until she falls asleep. Then early in the morning, when all is still quiet, Sweet Face moves her dresser and sneaks downstairs. She tiptoes back with the cat supplies she bought and puts him in the closet together with his food, water and a litter box she prepares. She makes a "Ssssh" sound with her finger to her lips. She closes the closet door and then shuts her bedroom door.

The cat crouches in a corner, sensing that his only fan is Sweet Face. As he eats his food and laps some water, he keeps a wary eye on the door. Sometime later, he's awakened when the closet door is thrown open, and there she is, Meanie! She throws a towel over the cat and thrusts him into a sack, which she ties shut. As Meanie races down the stairs. the cat hisses in defiance and tries, unsuccessfully, to claw his way out of the bag. He thinks, *Is she going to kill me? Will I ever see Sweet Face again?* Then the sack is tossed into the back seat of a car and Meanie drives off at a furious pace. When they stop, Meanie unties the sack and grabs the slashing ball of fur. He manages to give her hand one swipe with his claws before she tosses him out of the car, which then speeds away.

After landing with a thump, the cat looks at his scary, unfamiliar surroundings and then runs into an ally way and hides beside some boxes. He huddles against the wind that blows the grit around and licks himself where he stings from being thrown on the sidewalk. Normally he thrives on the street, but this place is out of his territory. To make things worse, it starts to rain. He climbs into an abandon crate and bristles in a corner against the wind and damp. In the morning, he ventures out to find some food and water. He laps some muddy liquid that has accumulated in a gutter and then goes in search of something to eat. All the people are in a hurry and rush by him. Most of his time is spent just trying to keep from getting stepped on. He then spots a man sitting on the ground who has a scraggly beard and wears old clothes. This dishevelled man throws something in the cat's direction who draws back in a defensive mode, but then the cat gets a whiff of meat. With caution, still remembering Meanie, he inches towards the offering. He finally grabs the morsel in his mouth and runs back to his hiding place. The cat thinks, *I don't know why he gave me that piece 'a meat, but I ain't gonna turn down food!*

The next day the cat repeats yesterday's actions. As he approaches, the man with the meat throws out another piece closer to himself. The cat's instinct says to back off, but the smell of the meat is irresistible, and he's still hungry. Creeping up, he grabs the meat. The man doesn't move, so the cat devours the morsel where it lands. He reasons, maybe this guy will be good for some more food. Then the man takes out a bowl, pours something white into it and offers it. The cat sniffs it, and it smells sweet. Taking a lick, it also tastes great. He thinks, *This reminds me of Mom's milk. I'm still not sure I trust this guy, and I certainly don't need him to survive. What do I call him? Let's see, hey! Meat Man 'cause he's good for some great eats.*

Vince: *In this story you're writing, is it believable that people like Meanie exist? How could a person treat an animal like that!*
Shakespeare: *From my conversations with cats, it happens more than you want to believe. I've even read newspaper accounts of people that drown kittens!*
Vince: *That's terrible. I guess that's why cats are so standoffish and take time to trust people.*
Shakespeare: *Exactly. That's one reason I want to write this book so people can see things from an animal's point of view. Anyway, my tale continues with an unlikely partnership.*

Chapter Three: An Unlikely Partnership

JOE THINKS, *IT WORKED! The milk gets him to trust me. Instead of running away, he stays put even though he looks at me with a quizzical stare. I wonder what he's thinking?* After a while, Joe decides to test the cat's intentions. He gets up and starts to leave. Joe wonders, *Will he follow me?* As Joe walks down the street, this cat, who seems to embody curiosity, follows, but at a respectful distance. Joe then moves to another busy street corner where he again puts out his cap. Joe sits and watches the cat who seems to shadow him, stopping and peering at him with caution. He decides to call this wary feline, Tom Cat, since the name fits the swagger in his walk as he struts around.

Joe begins his pitch to the passing crowd, "Help a veteran. Thank you, Mam'; have a good day."

After accumulating enough coins, he goes to the local fast food joint with Tom Cat following behind.

"Sorry buddy you have to wait outside," Joe tells Tom Cat.

When Joe comes out, Tom Cat is still there, licking his lips. Joe sits at a table the restaurant has set up outside and decides to see if Tom Cat is a real comrade or is *just in it for the food.* Joe puts a piece of meat in his lap and waits for Tom Cat's response. Tom Cat hesitates for a while, but then inches forwards. Finally, he comes onto Joe's lap and starts to eat. Slowly, Joe lifts his hand and pats him. Tom Cat backs away with a start, but then he returns in a slow, deliberate manner. Once again Joe starts to pat him, and this time Tom Cat doesn't move but just keeps on eating. With that, Joe figures he has a pal. At the end of the day, after Tom Cat and Joe have supper, they go back to Joe's spot on the hot air vent.

Chapter Four: Trust

TOM CAT SIZES UP MEAT MAN and decides, *Even though he don't look nothin' like Sweet Face, he has a good heart, and I think he just wants ta be my friend. Maybe I'll give him a chance and hook up with him. I certainly ain't had any better offers.* They stop at a place that has hot air blowing up from an iron mesh. Meat Man lays out a blanket, and they settle in for the night. Meat Man picks up Tom Cat and starts to stroke his fur. At first, Tom Cat bristles and scoots away. Meat Man persists and picks him up again and starts to pet him. This time Tom Cat has to acknowledge that it actually feels kind of good, though he doesn't want to admit it to Meat Man. Tom Cat thinks, *I'll let him stroke my fur if it makes him feel good, but only on my terms.* Meat Man finally covers them with a second raggedy blanket, and they both lie down for the night.

Tom Cat wakes up with Meat Man screaming. Tom Cat scrambles to his feet and scurries away. When he looks back, Meat Man has this wild expression on his face. Tom Cat wonders, *Maybe I misjudged him. Maybe I should just scram.* But then Tom Cat sees Meat Man put his hands to his eyes and starts to weep. At first Tom Cat is puzzled. Finally, he goes over to Meat Man and rubs against him. He begins to calm down and gently strokes Tom Cat, who starts to purr. Meat Man holds Tom Cat close, and Tom Cat can tell he's a comfort to him. Tom Cat senses, *My purring seems to relax Meat Man.* Eventually, they both go back to sleep and rest till morning.

Chapter Five: Redemption

JOE THINKS, *WHAT A ROUGH NIGHT. Bill's eyes haunted me again. Then I felt Tom Cat rubbing against me. His purring seemed to comfort me. It brought me back from my terror.*

"Thank God you were here. I'm not sure what I'd have done without you." Joe says to Tom Cat,

As Joe watches Tom Cat tilt his head. Joe says to him,

"I know you can't understand my words, but I think you know my meaning."

Joe wonders, *What's he doing now?* Joe then observes, *Oh, I see he's grooming himself.* As Joe rubs his chin he thinks, *Hmm. I could use a little sprucing up myself. I know there are some scissors and a mirror in my duffle bag somewhere.* Joe locates them and makes snips here and there on his unruly hair and beard. Joe then remarks to Tom Cat, "There now. You don't have to be ashamed to be seen with me."

On Joe's way to his begging spot, he makes a stop at a pet store to get something to occupy Tom Cat while he's pleading for his daily bread. When Joe and Tom Cat get to their destination, Joe pulls out his surprise, a bouncing ball on a string. To Joe's dismay, Tom Cat doesn't seem that interested in his toy – that is until some people come by. He then starts playing with it feverishly. People stop, especially people with children. They always leave a generous donation and tell Joe it's for his friend. Joe observes, *It's almost as if*

Tom Cat plays with the ball just to attract a crowd and get us more money. No! That can't really be, or can it?

When Tom Cat first sees that ball on a string he thinks, *No, not a dumb ball again.* But then he remembers that *cute* was what sold those stupid kittens, and he reasons, *If playing with that ball can get us more food, why not!* Tom Cat is amazed when it actually works!

As the crowd starts to accumulate, a man and a woman step forward and sit down beside Joe and Tom Cat. As Tom Cat keeps playing with the ball, the man starts to strum a tune on his guitar, while the woman begins to sing. The crowd keeps growing and growing. Joe notices that Tom Cat starts batting the ball in time with the music. Every time Tom Cat bats the ball, the crowd lets out a roar of approval. Joe's cap is showered with coins. A few folks even hand him some bills. Joe doesn't know what to say. The performance goes on all afternoon. Joe even gets up and does a little break dancing that draws some "Ahhhs" and then laughs when he falls; the money just keeps pouring in. After the crowd finally disperses, Joe offers his musical companions some of the money, but they shake their heads and tell him to just take care of his feline friend. After their show, both Tom Cat and Joe eat well. When they take their place on the heating vent, Tom Cat crawls up onto Joe's lap and starts to purr. Joe finds this so soothing that he becomes drowsy. Carefully placing Tom Cat beside him, Joe dozes off. When Joe wakes up in the morning, he feels so refreshed. It suddenly occurs to him that Bill's eyes have not haunted him. He's able to sleep peacefully for the next week. Tom Cat's purring seems to have exorcised all Joe's demons, and he no longer wakes up to the *terror of the night.*

Then it happens. They are sitting at their begging site as usual. Tom Cat is sunning himself while they wait for more passersby. Suddenly this huge mongrel appears from around the corner, grabs Tom Cat by the nape of the neck and starts to shake him. Joe takes his begging bowl and tosses it at the intruder, coins and all. Joe then jumps on him and tries to free Tom Cat. Joe punches the dog right in the face. The demon dog lets go of Tom Cat and bites Joe's arm instead. With his free hand Joe reaches out and finds a stray brick from a building that is being demolished and bashes the *hound from hell* over the head. He goes yelping off. Joe goes to Tom Cat. He's still breathing, and he meows faintly. Joe pick him up and flags down a taxi.

"Take me to the nearest vet's office," Joe yells. "I'll give you an extra five bucks if you make it quick."

Joe's just glad he is flush with money because of the previous begging sessions. They race for what seems like forever. When they pull up to the vet's office, Joe throws the money for the fare at the driver and then rushes inside.

"This is an emergency! You must save him," Joe screams. Fortunately, the office is not busy, so they show Joe and Tom Cat into an examination room right away. The vet comes in, and Joe explains what happened. She gently examines Tom Cat and listens to his heart.

"He's had a terrible shock. I can't feel any broken bones, but we'll have to take X-rays to be sure," the vet says with a sympathetic voice.

Joe replies, "You have to save him! You must, no matter what it takes!"

"We'll do all we can," she answers with a reassuring voice.

Joe waits for what seems like an eternity. When the vet comes out, she has a smile on her face.

"Your friend is very lucky. There are no broken bones, and he appears to have no internal injury. We're going to keep him overnight just to be sure."

Joe heaves a huge sigh of relief.

The vet continues, "But you should get that arm looked at."

"Oh, it's okay," Joe replies.

"Well, ethically I shouldn't, but I'll at least clean it up and bandage it."

Joe winces as she pours antiseptic on his wound and then applies a dressing. Joe heads back to the hot air grate, but it's with trepidation that he goes to sleep. After a restless night of tossing and turning, Joe rushes to the vet clinic as fast as he can. He's never been so happy as when the vet brings out Tom Cat, who starts his purring as soon as Joe takes him into his arms and thinks, *Thank God he's okay; however, I know we can't continue to live on the street. I must get a regular job and a place to stay inside, away from dog monsters that can kill Tom Cat. Next time we might not be so lucky!* Joe goes to a friend of his who owns a Bar and Grill.

"Hey, Jim," Joe says as he holds out his hand.

Jim replies in a hesitant manner, "How are ya doin' man?" not shaking Joe's hand.

Joe withdraws his hand and says, "I'm doing much better now, thanks to my friend here, Tom Cat."

"He's a bit scraggly, ain't he?"

"I was wondering if I could get a job washing and cleaning up."

"Yeah, but remember when you tried that once before; it didn't end so well.

"Things are completely different now. Thanks to Tom Cat I can sleep, and Bill's eyes no longer haunt me. Tom Cat's purring fixed all that."

"Well, I don't know."

"Please, I know I can do it now."

"Okay, but only because we're both vets from the same outfit. Hey, no drinking. I can't have you going crazy on me."

"I swear. Can I stay in the back room like before? I'll make sure no one breaks in."

"Okay. But no sampling my wares. I don't want to find you passed out in your own puke."

"No! Tom Cat will see to that!"

Thanks to Tom Cat, Joe can feel his life turning around. He sleeps more and more peacefully as he continues to receive Tom Cat's *purr therapy*. After a month, Jim sits down with Joe and hands him a soda pop.

"I gotta hand it to you. You really straightened out your life."

"It's all due to Tom Cat," Joe replies as he takes a swig of Coke.

"I ain't trying to get rid of you, but weren't you a crackerjack mechanic before you went into tha military."

"Yeah, I guess I was."

"Well I got a friend who runs a garage who's looking for a good mechanic. I'd hate to lose you, but he'll pay you a lot more than I ever can."

Before Joe applies for the job, he shaves, cleans himself up, and buys clean clothes. Now Joe just has one more thing to do to get his life back the way it was. He goes to the playground where his kids go after school. He can see Carrie going down a slide and Mark on the swings. As he approaches with Tom Cat, they suddenly recognized him, and come running.

"Daddy, Daddy," they yell.

Joe just can't help it. Tears come pouring out of him.

"Daddy, what's wrong?" the kids ask as they gather around.

"Daddy's fine. I'm just so happy."

"Daddy you have a cat. What's his name? Can we pet him?"

"He's a very special friend. He helped Daddy get better."

Tom Cat starts to purr as Joe's kids pet him.

"If you're better, can you come home? Can you Daddy?"

"Yes, Daddy will try."

Tom Cat observes: *Meat Man and the kids show up at this house that I guess must be his wife's. He talks quite a bit with this woman who comes to the door. We don't stay there right away. But our visits become more and more frequent. Finally, we moved in for good, and I have my new home. I often think about Sweet Face, and how she must miss me. I hope when she grows up she can find a kitty friend. As much as I loved Sweet Face, I think Meat Man needed me more.*

Vince: *As I read Shakespeare's story it brings tears to my eyes. From what I gather from my talks with my friend, Shakespeare's tale is not too far afield from what actually happened to him. That shows how good Shakespeare's intuition is. This story and others in this book demonstrate how therapeutic animals can be to those suffering from mental and physical ailments. I'm heartened to see that some hospitals and seniors' residences are starting to realize this fact and allow visits with animals.*
Shakespeare: *I am happy that Vince likes my story. I only hope that it will inspire even more people to realize how effective we animals can be in assisting humans get over rough patches in their lives.*

Tale Six: Skotch the Magnificent

Lauren and Skotch, "The Magnificent."

Vince: *Shakespeare's writing of this tale starts with a ring of our door bell. When I answer it, I'm surprised to see my daughter, Lauren.*

"Ah, come in. Your mothers out; we didn't know you were coming over," I say with a questioning look on my face.

Lauren: *"Oh that's okay. I actually came to see Shakespeare. He sent me a text asking me to drop by. He mentioned something about wanting my help writing a story for the book you guys are going to publish." Dad and I walk over to Shakespeare's cushion where he is sitting with his computer.*

Shakespeare: *I acknowledge Lauren with a woof, and type for her, "Yes, over the years I've been chatting with your horse, Skotch, and taking notes on your adventures with him. I think your partnership will make a great story in which you two are the main protagonists, and I can weave together both your's and Skotch's sides of this tale told in your voices.*

Vince: *Hey, as far as I know, Skotch and Lauren aren't protagonists; they get along fine.*

Shakespeare: *No! No! Protagonists just refers to the main characters in a story.*

Vince: *We've talked about this before. Why can't you just express yourself in everyday English!*

Shakespeare: *Yes. Being an erudite scholar, I sometimes forget to enunciate my thoughts in a plebian manner.*

Even though Vince rolls his eyes, I continue typing for Lauren, "What I want to do is write a story inspired by your relationship with Skotch—the healing power of the love you and Skotch feel and how it helps both of you through all your trials. You tell me what you remember, and I'll weave a story around it in your voice. In addition, I'll fill in what Skotch was thinking at the time based on notes recorded from my numerous conversations with him. I know it may be painful, but I would like to start with how you felt after losing your horse Zing, and how Skotch helped you cope with your grief."

Lauren begins to tear up a bit. I type to her, "It's okay if you don't want to do it right now," but she dries her eyes and begins relating her narrative while I start creating the story.

Chapter One: The Dark Cloud Lifts

Skotch helps Lauren heal.
They share many adventures.
But where will it end?

HEARTBREAK! THAT'S HOW this phase of my story begins as we are transported back in time to when I just lost Zing, my beloved horse. I begin this phase of my journey with my feelings, Blackness, like a cloak, keeps closing in on me. Ever since the death of Zing, my soul mate, I am sunk in a dark well and can't escape. It's all I can do to get up and eat. My dad, Vince, takes me to a doctor, and I take some pills the doctor prescribes. Then, on the way home, Dad surprises me by stopping at the stable where I rode Zing.

"Dad no! I can't do this. Take me home!" I plead.

"Come on Lauren, it will do you good to see your old friends. They've been calling a lot, asking how you are," my dad coaxes.

"I can't face them and the horses. They remind me too much of Zing," I scream and hold onto the door handle when Dad tries to pull me from the car. He eventually gives up, and when we get home, I run up to my room, slam the door and bawl 'til I have no more tears.

After a few weeks, my longing to see my riding friends begins to overcome my sadness and terror, though I'm not sure about facing the horses. I finally muster enough courage to ask Dad to take me to the stable. As we pull up and get out of the car, a strange thing happens. When we walk by a paddock, I can see the horse Skotch, whom I recognize from my days of riding at this stable. He seems to stare at me and then makes up his mind. He comes galloping and only stops when he is right next to me. He sticks out his giant head and starts nuzzling me. I embrace him and all the sadness and grief just pour out of me in a fountain of tears.

Shakespeare: *At this point Lauren breaks down and cries. I suggest we take a break, and Lauren goes to the bathroom. While she is composing herself, I have a chance to consult the relevant notes I typed up after my conversations with Skotch. Now being a Westphalian breed from Germany, Skotch is not easy to talk to. When I first try to converse with him, he looks a little startled and puts his nose up and turns away. Perhaps he thinks I'm a mutant horse, and it's beneath his dignity to address me. The only way I'm able to reach him is to get carrots from the barn and bring them to him while Lauren takes him out to graze. Thus, I finally penetrate his loftiness through his stomach! As haughty as Skotch is, he can be quite sentimental about those he likes as he shows in his recollection of his first encounter with Lauren after she returns to the stable.*

Skotch: *As soon as I see her, I recognize her. Though she has been gone for quite a while, I remember her for how she treated me and all my friends. Unlike some of the stable hands, when she cleaned out the stalls, she always made sure all the horses had fresh straw and would give us some sweet tasting little round disks she called mints. I was envious of her special friend she called Zing. She would take Zing out for grass and spend hours grooming and fussing over her. No one ever did that for me! It was a* *quick groom, put on the saddle and then out to the practice ring. Afterwards they would give me a quick bath and then right back into the stall. I would look out my window and see the other horses playing in the paddock. The humans never let me out; I guess they thought I was so fragile that I would break. But most of all, I remember watching her as she left after Zing died. She sobbed; she loved Zing so much. I wondered if anyone would ever love me that way, or would I always just be something for humans to use. I long for someone like Tender, which is the name I decided to give the little female human because she is so tender-hearted and loves us horses so much.*

Shakespeare: *After Lauren returns with some tissues to dry her eyes, she continues relating her recollections, and I weave them into a story.*

After seeing Skotch, I dry my eyes and remark to Dad while stroking Skotch's mane, "He remembers me. I'm sure of it."

"Yes, I think you're right. Just look at how he nuzzles you," Dad replies.

"Hi Lauren," says Mary.

I recognize her as she immerges from the stable as my old jumping coach from when I had Zing,

Mary exclaims, "I thought that was you. I see Skotch remembers you also."

"He came running right over, as soon as we pulled up," I reply.

"Yes, you always did have a way with horses. I think they must sense how much you love them," says Mary as she scratches Skotch's ears.

I then gather up enough courage to ask, "Can I help feed the horses today."

"Yes, of course, honey. You're always welcome. Why don't you bring Skotch in?" asks Mary, as she hands Skotch's lead line to

Lauren. "Mr. Morris, why don't you come along and grab a cup of coffee from the office?"

I spend the rest of the afternoon helping feed the horses and cleaning out their stalls. Seeing all my old equine friends and meeting a few new ones almost makes me forget Zing. However, when passing Zing's old stall, I can't help but linger. I shed a few tears and pat the stall like I'm saying goodbye. I spend a lot of time with Skotch, taking him out for grass and grooming him. I give him lots of hugs and kisses and also carrots and apples, which he gobbles up while smacking his lips.

I keep volunteering at the stable throughout the summer. One day as I'm cleaning out the stalls as usual, a well-dressed woman comes into the stable. I've seen her around a lot but was never introduced to her.

"Hello. I'm Mrs. Grayson. I own this riding stable."

"Hello," I reply and start to extend my hand, but pull it back when I see how dirty it is.

"I understand you've been working here all summer for free," says Mrs. Grayson.

"Well, I don't really consider it work. I just love being around horses.".

"Yes. Mary has been telling me about you. She's not easily impressed, but she can't stop raving about what a great worker you are. You never shirk when it comes to caring for the horses. I also heard about the tragedy with Zing. I'm so sorry."

I hesitate with my head bowed, but manage to blurt out, "Yes, I miss her so much."

"Well, we'll have to see what we can do about that," replies Mrs. Grayson with a wink of her eye. "In the meanwhile, I want to hire you to work here taking care of the horses. I also want to pay you for all the work you've already done."

I'm so thrilled I can't think what to say, but eventually I manage to blurt out my gratitude to Mrs. Grayson with a huge grin and some halting words. Later I receive the shock of my life. One day I'm working in the stable doing my daily chores when Mrs. Grayson and Mary come in and Mrs. Grayson asks Dad if he would mind joining them in the office. I'm about to burst with curiosity, but they close the door, so I can't hear what they're saying. When they come out, they all have big smiles on their faces. Mrs. Grayson speaks first.

"We've been talking with your dad. I understand that you've taken a real shine to Skotch."

"Yes, we've formed quite a bond. He especially likes it when I take him out for grass. When he nuzzles me, I think he's saying thank you," I reply, feeling like I'm about to explode with suspense.

"Yes, that's what I've heard." Mrs. Grayson says as she nods. "Well I've made a proposal to your dad. Now as you know, Skotch has been trained to high level dressage[17], and he's been up for sale since our Grand Prix[18] instructor, Gustave, got a new horse and is no longer showing Skotch. Well, we've been offered a lot of money for him and..."

"And...and, what?" I gasp.

Mrs. Grayson finally continues after what seemed an eternity, "But you know, money isn't everything. You remind me of myself when I was a girl. I loved the horses just the way I see you do. So,

---

17 Dressage is an equestrian discipline that teaches the rider to sift the horse's weight onto its hind legs while performing various movements and thus compensate for the rider's weight throwing the horse off balance

18 The highest level of dressage competition involving specified, advanced maneuvers.

I've offered to sell Skotch to you and your dad at a considerable discount provided you keep him here and take lessons from us."

I can't believe my ears. I turn wide-eyed to Dad. "Is it possible? Can Skotch be mine?"

Dad replies, "I'll have to check with your mom, but I think we can swing it."

I hug Dad and then run to Skotch's stall with a big bunch of carrots. I put my arms around his massive neck as he consumes his treats.

After the sale of Skotch is completed, I start taking regular dressage lessons on Skotch from Gustave. Occasionally, I'm also taught by Alana, who taught me dressage when I had Zing. She's Gustave's wife and an accomplished dressage rider herself. In the beginning, it's very difficult. Riding a small horse like Zing is very different from riding Skotch. I have to build up my muscles in my back and legs. After all, Skotch weighs more than ten times my weight. I struggle to get Skotch to carry his weight from behind and bend his body around my leg. However, gradually I begin to make progress.

Shakespeare: *At this point in her narrative Lauren complains her mouth is getting dry, and she goes into the kitchen for a drink. This gives me a chance to check my notes to see what Skotch thought of all this. He told me he felt very close to Tender. He could sense what she felt. He also recalls Tender's problems with riding him in the beginning, but he was just glad she was his rider despite all the problems. He also told me this was very different from the feelings many other horses had towards their riders. Skotch's words from my notes are:*

Skotch: *Whenever Tender holds me, I feel a real bond forming. In contrast, the other horses are laughing at their riders.*

The brown horse in the stall next to mine, I call Sensitive because she really hates it when her rider spurs and whips her, neighs out, "It took my rider a long time to get me under control. That will teach her to use spurs and a whip on me! She doesn't need to use them so hard. I'd obey a lot better if she just used a light touch."

The horse across from me, I call Boots because of his white legs, adds, "Yeah, my rider urges me to go forward and then jerks my reins and hurts my mouth when she can't keep up. Then she seems surprised when I rear."

A horse the others call Lucky out of sarcasm says, "You guys are the fortunate ones. My rider bounces on my back every time she tries to trot or canter me. I wonder how she'd feel if I bounced up and down like a lump on her back?"

I did sympathize with Lucky since it sounds like fate hasn't abided by his name when he gave him his rider. I personally view most of the humans that sit on our backs with great distain. I would only obey them because they give me no choice. The one exception is Tender. Because she treats me with nobility as I deserve, I never want to disappoint her. When my fellow horses point out all the problems Tender has when trying to ride me, I tell them that Tender has a good heart and is trying her best. They should wait and see. She'll be the best rider at this stable!

"That's not saying much," they all neigh derisively.

With that I begin to wonder what the riders would think if they could understand what their horses were saying about them! My thoughts then wander back to Tender. I recall that in the beginning it is difficult. I can tell that Tender is trying, but she is just not strong enough to shift my weight onto my hind legs. I am continuously out of balance, but slowly I can feel her strength and ability growing. She can even start to bend me around her leg. As we go down a line she can now, first bend my rear end out, then bring it back in line and then use her legs to push out my shoulders. This bending is an exertion for me, but I'm willing to try more for Tender than any other human. I'm more than just a performer to her. What I love most is how much time Tender spends with me. We go out for grass, and she sits looking at bound sheets of paper with scribblings on them unless I nuzzle her. Then she scratches my ears and hand-feeds me some grass. I'm so happy to be out in the fresh air and not stuck in that stuffy, old stall. I can tell the other humans make fun of my Tender when she's out with me, but she doesn't seem to care and neither do I. We will show them! I have a feeling that we will soon have our chance.

Shakespeare: *Skotch's premonition soon comes true. Lauren's riding on Skotch does continue to improve in a dramatic fashion until she is one of Gustave's best students, but Lauren always gives the credit to Skotch. Lauren returns and continues her story.*

I exclaim to Dad as I dismount from Skotch after our lesson, "Skotch is just so amazing! Did you see his shoulder in[19] and then his half pass[20]? I can't believe how great he is."

"I can also see how you've improved. You were good on Zing, but your riding has risen to a whole different level," Dad replies.

"No! It's all him." I protest, pointing to Skotch.

Just then Gustave and his wife come over. "We've been talking, and we think that you and Skotch are ready to enter a local show next weekend. You two have really improved."

"Skotch is ready, but am I?" I ask, patting Skotch.

"Yes, you've improved so fast since you started riding Skotch. Besides, it's a great chance for you and Skotch to get accustomed to showing together. We're aiming towards having you enter the Young Riders' Competition[21] to represent Ontario," says Gustave while Alana nods in agreement.

"Is that possible," I ask in disbelief.

---

[19] A movement in which the horse moves on three tracks with its shoulders bent to the inside.

[20] A lateral movement in which the horse is bent in the direction of travel.

[21] A competition for the best riders from 16-25 from different regions in the USA and Canada.. The competition includes riders who compete in dressage, stadium jumping or eventing.

Dad looks startled and asks, "I know Lauren is quite talented; she proved that with Zing. But competing in the Young Riders' Program is a whole different ballgame. Do you really think Lauren can do it?"

"Well, Skotch has done this all before, and he can serve as a schooling master to teach her. If Lauren continues to work as hard as she has been, I don't see why she can't."

I hug Skotch's neck and declare, "Yes! Skotch and I can do it. Just you wait and see!"

But it's first things first. The beginning step for us is to compete in a local show. Alana and Gustave think that the medium level is an appropriate class for us. Skotch and I work extremely hard right up to the day of the show. As is our habit, Dad and I arrange for a stall at the stable where the show is to be held. On the day of the competition, we have Skotch trailered to the show site. After Skotch is settled in his stall with lots of water and hay, my family and I have supper and go right to bed, since my riding test is scheduled for 10:05 AM. The next morning we arrive early at the stable, and I feed Skotch his hay and grain. Dad then helps me groom Skotch. As he picks the dirt and manure out of Skotch's hooves I ask,

"How many times have you done this for Zing and now Skotch?"

"I don't know. I've lost track, but I wish a dime came my way for each hoof," Dad exclaims!

I laugh and continue grooming Skotch.

"Okay Dad, it's time for me to start braiding Skotch's mane."

Dad remarks as he hands me some white tape, "I don't know how you do it, but the way you incorporate white yarn into his braids and then wrap them with white tape makes him look amazing."

"Yes, I have to admit it. This way of braiding his mane does make him look so handsome," I remark as I step back and look in admiration. The braids do show off Skotch's muscled neck so well that I just have to give him a hug. But then it's time for me to change into my competition clothes and take Skotch out to the warm-up ring. From my previous riding experience, I know that the warm-up is the most important part of the competition, particularly since all the competitors have to ride at a preassigned time. If you start the warm-up too soon, then the horse will be so worn out he can't do his best. Even worse is if you start too late, and the horse's muscles are not properly warmed up; not only will the horse not perform well, but you risk injury to your horse. What's even trickier is that the optimal warm-up time is different for each horse and can change from competition to competition, even for the same horse. As I mount Skotch, a familiar yell rings out. It's Alana.

"Alright Lauren, It's time to start your warm-up in earnest."

Shakespeare: *Okay Lauren, you can take a break now. I want to fill in Skotch's view on the competition from my notes. Lauren stretches, and Vince suggests they both go into the kitchen to get a drink and a snack. I find the appropriate place in my notes and start to record events from Skotch's vantage:*

Skotch: *As soon as I see Tender coming with my halter and leading me out to the trailer, I know something is up. When we arrive at the show grounds my suspicions are confirmed. Yes, it's a competition. I remember thinking, I should have guessed it, the way we were working with such intensity for the last several weeks. Competitions make me so nervous. I get a little queasy in my stomach and that sometimes affects my performance. For most riders it doesn't matter to me, but I never want to disappoint Tender. After we arrive at the show, Tender leads me into a stall. As I start munching from my hay net, I again think, Tender is so considerate. She makes sure I have lots of hay, and I can tell from the taste that she takes care that my feed is from home, so I won't get a belly ache. She is so thoughtful.*

The next day, after Tender finishes fussing over me, it's time to go out into the show ring. This is old hat for me, but I know that competing at this level against these horses could be intimidating to Tender, since I mainly saw her practice jumping with Zing. As we start the warm up, a competitor horse neighs in contempt and tries to throw me off my paces. This comes as no surprise to me since I've seen it all before, so I just proceed on. Just as my muscles are warmed up, Lauren walks me out to the show ring. I can see the white fenced area where the test will be. There are people in little huts that are always there at every show. I think they are judges, because in the past, one of them in each hut always is talking as I perform my movements, and the other person appears to be scribbling on something. On the way to the competition ring, I can feel Tender starting to tense up. The previous horse has just finished as we enter the area outside of the ring. I put on the most high-stepping and active trot I can manage since, from experience, I know the initial impression of the judges is key to having my rider be happy. Finally, a bell rings, and I enter the ring at a trot. I can tell that Tender is still nervous, but I try my utmost. Tender takes over and gives signals for all my movements. After the initial halt in the center of the ring, Tender calls for some bending at trot in the form of circles. Bending has always been hard for me, but I strive to oblige Tender's commands. I can feel that Tender is happy with my effort. Tender then has me do an extended trot. We just fly across the ring. We then halt and go backwards. I start to veer sideways, but her legs keep me straight. I sense that she is finally getting over her nerves and starting to focus! I can feel her pushing more of my weight on my hind end. During the walk sequence, she is really urging me forward, so my back hooves extend as far forward as I can make them go. From her pats during our training I know Tender loves it when I do that. I then take up the canter. My weight is now completely being carried by my hind end, and my front end becomes so light. We then follow a serpentine pattern down the center line. Half way down I go into a walk, so I can pick up the correct canter lead[22]. I do some bending circles at canter and change my lead[23] while still cantering before I go back to trot and come down the center line for a final halt. After we finished the crowd applauds and Lauren gives me a big hug and pats me. I think we did okay because everyone seems to be very happy as we leave the competition ring. As I pass the horse that had been so rude in the warmup ring I whinny, "Let's see you beat that!" Later at the awards ceremony, I take more than a little satisfaction in noting that this bad actor is not present while I am!

Shakespeare: *Lauren and Vince come back with drinks in their hands. I go and get a drink from my water dish. Lauren indicates that she's ready to start again, so I ensconce myself on my cushion with my computer and start typing in her voice as she relates what she remembers after she finishes her competition.*

"Lauren, I'm so proud of you," yells Dad and Alana simultaneously as Skotch and I come out of the ring.

"It was all Skotch," I reply hugging and patting Skotch from my saddle.

Later on, as I'm grooming Skotch before putting him away in his stall, Alana come rushing up full of excitement.

"Don't undo Skotch's braids. You're in second place so far," she exclaims oozing pride.

It turns out Skotch and I finished third, which is thrilling considering there were twenty very experienced dressage riders in the class. At the award ceremony, all the winners are lined up mounted on their horses. When the official tries to put the ribbon on Skotch's bridle, he immediately works to get it in his mouth. The official shows wisdom by removing it and just handing it to me. I remark to the judge, "Skotch has the most talented mouth I have

[22] In the canter the horse's inside legs lead in a true canter.

[23] Change lead so the opposite legs leads.

ever seen." He smiles in reply. Skotch is probably not the first horse he has seen try to eat a ribbon!

I then dismount and lead Skotch back to his stall. He uses his lips like a pickpocket to try to get at the treats I have in my pocket. His action reminds me of a time early one morning when Dad and I go out to the stable. Skotch has managed to undo the catch on his stall door with his dexterous lips. We find Skotch on Mrs. Grayson's front yard where he is busy eating the grass; horses are never allowed to graze there. Just as I run up to Skotch to grab him by the halter, Mrs. Grayson comes out in her house coat.

"Oh, I'm so sorry Mrs. Grayson. I don't know how he got out," I recall apologizing with sheepish, down turned eyes.

I also remember Mrs. Grayson's gracious response, "Oh that's okay honey; he's always doing that. I'm just surprised he waited this long to do it while you own him."

But now my thoughts wander to the most embarrassing thing Skotch ever did. I have told this story many times, and it always gets a gasp of horror and then a big laugh. It occurs one night while Mrs. Grayson is having a big party at her house. She loves to put on big galas with the men dressed in their tuxedoes and the ladies in their finest ball gowns. During these parties, Mrs. Grayson tends to bring her guests down to the stable to show off the horses. Well, during one of these fancy affairs, I happen to be in the barn finishing up with an evening feed for the horses. Mrs. Grayson, wearing a silver ball gown with a long string of pearls, leads a procession of ladies and gentlemen into the stable. I feel quite out of place in my jeans, checkered shirt and scuffed work boots, so I try to be as inconspicuous as possible. All goes well until Mrs. Grayson arrives at Skotch's stall. To my horror, she slides opened Skotch's stall door and lets him poke out his huge head. The little bit of devil in Skotch couldn't let him miss this opportunity. He immediately grabs the front of Mrs. Grayson's dress and the pearls with his teeth and gives them a huge tug. The gown rips down exposing her underwear, and the pearls go flying everywhere. Watching in utter terror, I think I'm going to die. Visions of being banished from the stable and my poor parents having pay a fortune for the damages tortures me. We might not even be able to afford to keep Skotch. I wonder how he could be so naughty! I drop my scoop I've been using to feed the horses and fall to my knees in front of Mrs. Grayson trying to gather up as many of the pearls as possible. It isn't until I managed to scoop up about half of them that I hear Mrs. Grayson laughing, despite the horror on the faces of her guests.

"It's okay dear. I love how mouthy he is. Why do you think I bought him in the first place?" chuckles Mrs. Grayson as she grabs the front of her torn dress to cover up her chest.

Whenever I tell this story I always recall the lesson it taught me: a real horse person is not just someone who rides horses. This person knows what a privilege it is to befriend a horse!

As spring turns into summer, the typical rainy weather abates, and everyone enjoys warmer, sunny days. Thus Skotch and I can ride in the outside training ring. I love the view of the verdant valley with the green rolling hills and forest areas dotting the landscape that is visible from the ring. The pastoral scene is so idyllic. As the summer wears on, Skotch's and my training becomes more and more intense. One element of our riding becomes a secret just between Skotch and me. Every once in a while, we sneak out to a back field that isn't visible from the main stable. There's an oval track there that was used in the training of eventing horses[24]. Here I ride Skotch at a gallop. Feeling such power between my legs and the wind sailing by my face is exhilarating. I always thought Zing was

---

[24] Horses that take part in competitions consisting of dressage, cross country riding, and stadium jumping.

fast, but the dynamo that is Skotch is like riding a locomotive. Skotch seems to love it also. It's such a change from the confining, collected work that he is so used to in the training ring. I know that Gustave and Alana would have a heart attack if they saw Skotch and me racing around the track. They are so protective of Skotch. They fear that something would happen to him if he's allowed to do what horses love to do, run free. I decide that giving Skotch this pleasure will then allow him to better perform in the ring. It lets him blow off all his pent-up energy, so he can relax during a competition.

As the weather becomes warmer, Skotch and I start our training early in the morning or in the evenings to avoid the heat of the day. We also enter more shows. We're always in the ribbons, and even begin to win some of the classes we enter. Then as we start to win more and more competitions, we move up to competing at the highest medium level and start to win there also. One day Mrs. Grayson puts her arm around me and asks,

"Lauren, I'm wondering if you could do me a favor."

I stop brushing Skotch and reply, "Of course, Mrs. Grayson, I'm happy to do whatever I can."

"I'm on the board of our local hospital, and I'm wondering if you can put on a demonstration riding Skotch for some of the patients," she asks while giving Skotch a pat.

"I'll be honoured to," I agree while smiling broadly.

"Can you do it next Saturday morning? Oh, and will you wear your show outfit. I've arranged for one of Gustave's students to describe your movements."

So next Saturday, Dad and I arrive early and get Skotch ready. He looks magnificent in his braids. I don my competition blouse and jacket, white show pants, riding gloves, black boots and top hat. After warming Skotch up in the inside arena, I walk him to the outside ring where the demonstration will take place. The patients and staff are already there awaiting our arrival. There are many patients in wheelchairs. One of these that particularly catches my eye is a little girl that looks to me like she has cerebral palsy. This girl is so excited to see Skotch that she's bouncing up and down in her wheelchair. As Skotch trots down the center line of the show ring, I decide to open my ride with a flourish. Skotch rounds the first corner and flies across the diagonal in an extended trot with his front legs flashing out. That movement draws some gasps and then applause from the audience. I next signal for some bending work that includes half passes. When Skotch goes sideways with both his front and back legs crossing over, the crowd roars its approval. I now have Skotch take up a canter and finish the demonstration with flying changes[25]. When we finish, I take Skotch back into the barn to wash the sweat off him while the others retire to Mrs. Grayson's house for some desserts. As I just complete hosing Skotch off, I hear a timid voice.

"Ahh Ma'am, we really enjoyed your performance. It is all Amy can talk about since you finished."

I look down, and there is the little girl I had noticed earlier, with her mother. The girl's eyes are sparkling as she holds out her hands. The mother continues with an apologetic tone in her voice. "Do you think it would be possible for Amy to pet your horse? It would mean so much to her."

"Well...I don't know. He is pretty mouthy," I reply with a wary expression.

But before I can move, Amy maneuvers her wheel chair right up to Skotch and touches his nose. Holding my breath in apprehension, I have visions of Skotch grabbing the girl in his mouth and lifting

---

[25] Lead changes while the horse remains at canter. The horse can appear to be skipping when performing several flying changes in a row.

her right out of her chair! But I need not have worried. Skotch is on his best behavior.

Shakespeare: *I consult my notes at this point since what Skotch told me about this encounter had slipped my mind. I am quite curious about his reaction. Oh yes, now I remember.*

Skotch: *I see this little human in front of me, but I can't figure out why she keeps sitting in that chair. I sense she wants to come over to me, but what happens next is a complete surprise. She comes right up to me, chair and all. My instinct is to rear or back away, but then she puts her hand on my nose. I instantly know she means no harm. She just keeps petting me and squealing in delight. I can see light coming into her eyes as they meet mine. Our souls just seem to meet on a level that transcends our differences. I don't usually respond to strangers, especially if we have not been formally introduced, but I must admit, seeing so much joy in her face brakes through my reserved nature. Tender look both relieved and overcome with happiness. When the little girl leaves, Tender gives me such a big hug and feeds me apples and carrots. I'm not sure why, but I never question a gift treat!"*

Shakespeare: *With that I call it quits for the day. It's time for my dinner and my walk with Vince. I type a good night to Lauren, and we agree to meet tomorrow.*

Shakespeare: *The next day Lauren comes over with some pictures of her and Skotch. She, Vince and I all sit down and look at them. The way Lauren caresses each picture before showing them to us is so indicative of her love and devotion. I can see a look of proud admiration on Vince's face as he watches Lauren. One picture shows Lauren in her competition finery sitting on Skotch with his mane braided. I ask, "Can we use this picture for our book?" She replies, "Of course." After we look at all the photographs, I suggest to Lauren that we continue with our story where she enters the Young Riders' Competition. So, the tale continues in Lauren's voice.*

Chapter Two: The Young Riders' Competition

MY HAND QUIVERS AS I HOLD the letter in front of the mail box. I hesitate, but finally drop it in. After the last regular show I enter, at the prompting of Alana and Gustave, I wrote this letter to the equestrian center in Toronto requesting to enter the North American Young Riders' Competition with Skotch. This decision is a daunting one since this program requires riding a special set of maneuvers that is similar to the ones ridden at the Pan Am Games, at four different recognized shows in Ontario. The top riders from Ontario compete against riders 16–25 from other Canadian provinces and the United States. It's all very exciting, but it's also very scary. Skotch and I will be competing against the best of the best. Later, I meet my competitors for the first time at a little drama that plays itself out at the home of the organizer, Mrs. Adams, who lives in Toronto. We all introduce ourselves and describe our riding experience. I discover that most of the girls are from the Toronto area and apparently know each other very well, since they have taken part in the same competitions for years. Three of them form a clique that seems to be led by Melissa, who looks at me with sideway glances like I'm an outsider who doesn't belong there. However, one girl named Penny comes right over to me with a grin and shakes my hand. Another girl named June doesn't come over, but does not join Melissa and her crew in their obvious hostility. She also seems to be shunned by the clique. I smile at her from across the room. June manages to smile back, but still does not join Penny and me; thus, we two sit together munching on cookies and drinking juice through the description of the program. During this presentation, Mrs. Adams informs us that we six riders are competing for four spots on the Ontario team. At the end, Penny and I exchange phone numbers and wish each other well, while Melissa and her gang glare at us.

Since Dad and I are in Toronto for the Young Riders' meeting anyway, we stop off at a tack store to get an appropriate riding jacket to wear when riding at the FEI[26] level. Our home tack stores don't carry jackets for riding at this level. Fortunately, the store we stop at has the jacket in my size.

I declare to Dad, "Isn't this the most exquisite jacket you've ever seen! Look at the gold buttons and long tails that even have little weights at their tips to keep them from flying up when I ride. I can't believe I get to wear such a fancy outfit."

Dad picks up an elegant top hat and hands it to me.

"Here try this on to complete your look. Oh, and we should get you a new gold-coloured collar pin to match the gold buttons on your jacket."

Dad appears to enjoy watching me strut around in my new riding clothes as much as I do. When we get home, I model my riding outfit all over again for Mom. This time I show off my new purchases with all my other riding gear. I prance back and forth in my dark navy blue riding coat, white blouse, pants and gloves, and

---

[26] Fédération Equestre Internationale – An International equestrian federation that governs international horse competitions.

black top hat together with my black knee length riding boots. These riding clothes really appeal to my vanity. I can hardly wait to wear my outfit while seated on Skotch the Magnificent (as I call him) with his white taped braids.

It seems like an eternity, but finally the time for the first Young Riders' Competition is at hand. At the stable, Mom, Dad and I pack a trunk with all the gear needed for the competition, including Skotch's saddle, bit, and reins. We also load grain and hay from our home stable to prevent Skotch from developing colic due to unfamiliar feed. Then Skotch is loaded into a horse trailer. When we arrive at the show grounds, I settle Skotch in his stall, and after dinner we all go to our motel.

The next morning starts out okay. The sun is shining, and there isn't a cloud in the sky. A fresh breeze is blowing; it is perfect riding weather. However, after we arrive at the stable, things start to go wrong. Braiding Skotch's mane is only half way finished when I discover that I haven't brought enough white tape to wrap his braids. Penny doesn't have any extra, and I know better than to ask Melissa and her clique for any, so I skip taping the braids. The next thing that happens is the new collar pin breaks, so I have to use a plain safety pin. I'm almost in tears when I don my riding clothes before taking Skotch out to the warm-up ring.

Dad puts his arm around me and with reassuring words says, "Everything's going to be okay once you get Skotch out to the warm-up area."

I think, *Dad always tries to have a calming influence on me during a crisis.*

When Skotch and I arrive at the warm-up ring, I receive another shock. Alana is not there to help me. After about fifteen minutes I can't wait any more and must start the warm up without her. I've never ridden this test through, so I'm quite nervous. A rider never actually rides the full test in practice, so the horse doesn't anticipate the moves; thus, only portions of the test are ridden at any one time. A thought haunts me, *What if I forget part of the test and have to withdraw?* I try to warm up Skotch the best I can, but my inexperience makes it hard for me to determine what work he needs to get him supple enough for the test. I'm gripped with panic when Dad tells me that it's time to go to the show ring. As we make our way to the ring, Alana comes running up.

"Oh Lauren, I'm so sorry. My car broke down, and I just got here."

As I start to ride around the outside of the ring while the judges are tallying the score for the previous rider, I can tell that with all the waiting for Alana, I started the warm up too late and Skotch is still stiff. When the bell rings Skotch trots down the center line to the first halt. I sense Skotch is not carrying his weight on his hind end, and his legs are not lined up properly for his initial halt. The three judges in their huts at the end of the ring facing me are whispering in an animated manner to their recorders. This fixation by the judges is not a good sign, since they are certain to note all the mistakes and thus give me a low score. At my command, Skotch then trots to the end of the ring and turns right, I start to do some bending work with him. He seems to relax more and get into the test; his confidence increases mine. I notice that the judges seem to be commenting less to their recorders, a good sign. I next guide Skotch into an extended trot, which is one of his strengths. We are really beginning to gel, when disaster hits! Someone on the show grounds turns on a deep-fat fryer. Its noise sputters, crackles and explodes into the hushed silence of the show ring and sends Skotch into frenzy, rearing and bucking!

Shakespeare: *At this point I suggest we take a break because I want to refer to my notes concerning Skotch's reaction to these events. Lauren sits* *back and relaxes with her pictures while I write about the test from Skotch's point of view as he remembered it.*

Skotch: *From when I first wake up, I can tell this is not going to be a good day. It's hard to explain. I wasn't sick. I just felt kind of "blaah," uninspired. When Tender comes into my stall to get me, I can sense that she's uneasy, and her mood begins to unsettle me even more. By the time she's ready to take me out to the practice ring, she shows signs of being a nervous wreck, which does nothing to increase my self-confidence. During the warm up, I can't understand why Tender seems to lack her ability to loosen me up. Then I notice someone is missing. Usually a woman is always there giving instructions to Tender. Before I feel completely ready, we start for the show ring. I'm not totally warmed up, but how can I let Tender know? Why must we go right now? When we start down the center line of the show ring, we are both stiff. Things start to get better as we go along, and then it happens. A blast sounds like someone is trying to kill me! I'm rearing and bucking before I even know what happened. I can feel that Tender is barely able to hang on. The last thing I want to do is to hurt her; she is so kind to me, but I can't help it. Even after we calm down, neither of us seem able to continue the test. We both exit the ring with our heads down in defeat.*

Shakespeare: *When I finish, Lauren and Vince both read what I have written. It brings tears to Lauren's eyes, and Vince remarks, "Yes, that was a real low point for all of us. But I was so proud of Lauren that she didn't quit the Young Riders' Program even though I'm sure she wanted to."*

I can see the pride in Vince's eyes and sense the love he has for Lauren. He tells me, "Lauren's determination despite this bitter memory is apparent when she says she's ready to start again with the second Young Riders' competition, without any prompting from me."

Lauren begins telling me how she felt and what she remembers after leaving the ring, and I start writing again.

Exiting the ring, I can see Melissa and her cohorts pointing and snickering at me. Right then the shame and hurt is unbearable, and I'm ready to quit. Mom, Dad and Alana try to comfort me, but to no avail. A dark cloud hangs over my head. To my surprise, when I put Skotch away, I can see a defiance in his eyes. His look means so much to me. Now I know I can't let him down by quitting. We are all silent on the way home. There is really nothing to say. I know my folks feel bad for me, but there's nothing they can do or say. It's really up to Skotch and me.

The next morning, there's a surprise phone call. It's from June. I guess she must have got my number from Mrs. Adams. She won the Young Riders' test on her beautiful horse, Champion, that she rides so expertly. I don't really want to talk to her or any of the other Young Riders, but I don't want to be rude.

"Hello, Lauren?"

"Yes." I suspect she's calling to gloat over her win.

June responds, "I'm sorry we didn't get a chance to talk at the show. I want to tell you that it's so unfair what happened to you. Some people are so careless. I know how devastating it can be because I had something similar happen to me last year. Please don't get discouraged. I really hope you'll be at the next show."

I don't know what to say but blurt out, "Thanks. Yes, I plan to go. Thanks for your call."

Thus, when the time for the second Young Riders' Test comes, I'm determined that Skotch and I will do better!

Shakespeare: *I always like to get Skotch's reaction to riding tests in addition to Lauren's. It's rare for a horse's voice to be heard. As both Lauren and Skotch tell me, communication between horse and rider is key for a good test; I think it's vital to get both points of view. Thus, I begin to* *write from my notes from Skotch on the second Young Riders' Test that took place two weeks later.*

Skotch: *When Tender mounts me I can feel how self-assured she is. We have such a close bond; I can sense these things. It's as if Tender and I can read each other's minds. When we enter the show ring, I lift my legs high and prance around the outside of the fenced area until the bell rings. As we go by the huts, the judges start to pay attention, like we are a pair to watch. When we go down the center line, I can feel Tender's seat push my back legs under me, helping me to make our halt square and in a line. Tender then pushes her inside leg against my side helping me to bend as we do our flexibility movements. Afterword, Tender signals me to halt and go back for five steps. I never quite understand why she wants me to do this, but I do my best to oblige. No sooner have I completed my steps back, when her legs squeeze my sides asking for a trot, so off we go again. As we go onto the diagonal, Tender squeezes even harder, and we sail to the other end with my front legs shooting out straight in front of me. It's exhilarating. We then go into our walk. Tender pushes as hard as she can so my stride is as long as possible without me going into a trot. Now we start our canter work and change the lead every fourth stride. Then we do that every third stride. Oops, I missed one. Oh well, we must go on. Finally, we come to our half turns on the spot, while I still keep up the canter with my hind legs[27]. Oh, oh, that last stride was more of a hop than a canter, but we can't stop now. As we go down the center line and do our final halt, I can sense relief in Tender. We've done it. It wasn't perfect, but we finished the entire test."*

Shakespeare: *I see a smile on Lauren's face as I show her Skotch's memories of this test. They were obviously both happy with it. Lauren and I continue with the tale in Lauren's voice.*

---

[27] A half pirouette.

"We did it! We did it!" I can't help but exclaim.

Alana, Mom and Dad all congratulate me as I walk Skotch back to the stable after dismounting.

"It was all Skotch," I declare and give him lots of pats and hugs. "He listens to me so well."

When the competition is over, June and Penny both come over.

"Congratulations on your test," they both exclaim while hugging me.

June wins again and Penny is third. Melissa is fourth. Even though I'm still last, I only finish a few points behind fourth and fifth. I see Melissa and her gang huddling in a corner, not looking quite as smug as they had before. The third and fourth shows went pretty much the same as the second show. I'm resigned to the fact that I won't make the Ontario team, when I receive an unexpected phone call from the head of the Young Riders' program.

"Hello Lauren, this is Mrs. Adams."

"Yes," I reply in a shy tone.

"First I want to thank you for taking part in the Young Riders' program. I also want to tell you that there is the possibility for you to go to the Young Riders' Championship after all. British Columbia does not have enough Young Riders to make up a team, and they are asking if one of our riders might like to compete with them. So, I'm wondering if you would like to be on their team?"

"What about the fifth-place rider?" I ask.

"I've already talked with her, and she says that if she can't be on the Ontario team, then she doesn't want to go."

I don't say anything to Mrs. Adams, but I think, *That sounds like one of Melissa's crew.*

I then respond to her invitation,

"Yes! Oh, I have to ask my folks first."

After I explain the situation to Mom and Dad, they agree. I can't help but yell out loud over and over,

"Skotch and I get to go to the Young Riders' Championship!"

I'm so excited that I can't stop jumping up and down. Mrs. Adams also explains that Skotch and I can travel with the Ontario team even though we are actually going to compete against them. After all this exciting news, I just have to call Penny.

"Penny did you hear? I get to go the Championships after all."

"That's wonderful Lauren. I'm so happy for you!...But how?"

"I'm going to be riding on British Columbia's team, but we can still pal around together."

"Yes, that's great. I'm glad you'll be there, so I don't have to face the Melissa mob by myself."

My next call is to June who is equally happy. It's great that I'll have at least two friends there. I know the show is big, but I have no idea how big until my credentials arrive in the mail together with a description of all that the show entails. This competition includes not just the top young dressage riders from the United States and Canada, but also the top stadium jumpers and event riders. It lasts for a week and is considered on the same level as the Pan Am Games. All the riders arrive on a Monday. On Tuesday, there is a mandatory inspection of all the horses. This is critical because, if the vets find anything at all wrong with your horse, you are out of the competition before you even have a chance to show. Wednesday and Thursday are the team championships. On Friday the top twenty riders compete in the individual riders' championship, and on Saturday is the award ceremony.

When I arrive at the show grounds, I see that, instead of stables, all the competitors are housed in a big tent with temporary stalls set up for each horse. Skotch is stabled with British Columbia's team, so I must bid Penny and June good bye. After making my way to Skotch's stall, I meet my teammates from British Columbia.

They're all friendly, but one member, Gwen, is especially nice. Gwen and I soon discover that we are both devoted to our horses and not just the competition. Later Penny and June also accept Gwen as a friend as soon as they met her, as I knew they would. Thus, I have three great buddies when facing the trials of the week. But now it's time to get Skotch settled into his stall and assemble my gear for the vet check tomorrow. While unpacking, I can hear a hammering coming from the stall behind me. When I go to check, a woman is trying to nail up a fan, so it will blow air on her horse. I'm not happy with the noise but don't want to complain. Next, I fetch Skotch some water. Just as I arrive back at the stall, there is a scream and a crashing sound. I rush over to the other side of the stall and see Skotch's immense head peering over the stall and the devastation I assume he has caused.

"I'm so sorry," I apologize while removing the ladder and fan from the lady.

"That horse tried to attack me. He should be locked up," the woman yells while pointing an accusing finger at Skotch, who looks quite sheepish. "I'm going to have him removed from the tent and kicked out of the competition. He's a menace," the women further threatens.

Fortunately, several people who happened to be passing by and saw the whole incident speak up.

"Hey, it isn't the horse's fault. All he did was look over to see what all the racket was. Besides, you should know better than to be hammering around horses."

With that, the woman stomps off in a huff. The people who spoke up tell me they will be happy to vouch for my horse, and they give me their names and show me where their horses are stabled.

I never hear from that woman again. But as I often remark, "With Skotch there's one thing you can always count on – there is never going to be a dull moment."

The first big hurdle of the competition is the vet check. It's a formal affair, so I get up early to groom and braid Skotch. I then put on my show outfit and wait in line for my turn. Alana, who agreed to come and help me, together with Mom and Dad, are in the audience. Dad has his usual very worried expression on his face. He always frets more than me at competitions. This concern doesn't help me with my nerves, but I realize that he can't help it. That's just the way he is.

For the inspection, first the vets look over the horses literally from their hooves up to their teeth. Any sign of cuts or other problems would immediately eliminate the horse. Of course, all the reins, bits and other equipment must adhere strictly to the rules. They then ask the rider to trot their horse away from the vet panel and then walk them back. One funny step and the horse can be subject to elimination. The horse just ahead of me doesn't pass the trot test. The judges send the poor girl and her horse off to a paddock for a retest after all the other horses have finished. If the horse fails again, then they are out. Tears well up in her eyes as she leads her horse away. This horse did have a slight stumble during his test, but he looked okay to me. It brings home how strict these vets are. Then it's my turn. I'm so affected by the fate of the previous competitor that I'm shaking. The vets go over Skotch and his tack and then ask me to trot him out. Just then Skotch notices my watch and decides to grab onto it. He literally lifts me off the ground by my watch band!

Shakespeare: *Once again I have to get Skotch's reaction from my notes.*

Skotch: *"I don't know what happened. I see the sun shining off this disk on Tender's wrist, and I can't resist grabbing that band attached to it. I hear a gasp rising from the crowd and see the terror in Tender's eyes, so I let go. A man then barks out the same order he had given before and Tender, with a very determined look on her face, starts me trotting down a* *line and then walks me back. The man in charge barks out a single sound, and Lauren and everyone else give a sigh of relief. As Tender leads me away, she is laughing. Apparently, my curiosity hasn't caused dire consequences."*

Shakespeare: *I now need to compare Lauren's reaction.*

As I lead Skotch back to the barn, I can't believe what happened. Why had Skotch picked that very moment to be mouthy? But as he nuzzles me, I can't be mad at him. That's just Skotch being Skotch. As Alana, Mom and Dad join me, we have a good laugh. All the horses on both British Columbia's and Ontario's team pass the vet check, so everyone goes onto the Team Competition. Unfortunately, I didn't see the number of the horse that failed the first time among those who passed. I felt so sorry for the rider.

Penny and June ride on the first day of the Team Test, but Gwen and I aren't scheduled until the second day, so we go shopping at some merchandise tents set up on the show grounds. I find a collar pin with a horse head on it that looks just like Skotch. I just have to have it to wear tomorrow for luck. Gwen buys a new pair of blue riding pants and a white blouse.

"They look quite stunning on you," I comment while Gwen looks in the mirror.

"Gee thanks, I'm so happy you came on our team; otherwise, I wouldn't have anyone else to pal around with."

"What about the other girls on our team?" I ask while we pay for our purchases.

"They're nice, but they're both from Vancouver and stick to themselves," Gwen replies while we walk back to where our horses are stabled.

"Would you like to stop in here and get a coffee and maybe a muffin?" I ask pointing to a food tent we pass.

"Sure," Gwen replies, putting her bags down by her seat.

After we buy our food, Gwen comments. "That horse of yours is a real character, isn't he?"

"Yes. He's quite the rascal, but that's why I love him so much."

"I thought so," comments Gwen. She then munches on a donut and drinks some coffee. After finishing her donut, she pulls out a picture of her horse, Rose.

"Your horse is such a beautiful mare. Her black coat sets off her four white feet so well. She has such kind eyes and temperament," I comment in admiration.

"Yes. She's a real sweetheart. I'm really lucky to have her," replies Gwen as she rubs the picture and gives it a kiss.

"Why do you say you're lucky to have her?" I query.

Gwen begins her story as she continues to caress the picture of Rose, "I grew up on a farm, and we always had pets around, but my folks aren't well off, so we could never afford a horse. But lucky for me, we live next to a horse farm owned by Mr. and Mrs. Jones, or Marty and Grace as they always tell me to call them. They are almost like family to my folks and me. They don't have any children, so they sort of adopted me. I'm always over at their house helping take care of their horses. Marty and Grace must be pretty well off because they have the most beautiful riding horses that they sell to jumping and dressage competition riders. One evening our doorbell rings. It's Marty, and he says something special and wonderful is happening. He asks if I want to come see. I ask my folks, and they nod approval. We go to Marty's and Grace's barn; as we walk down the aisle, we pass by stalls with their inquisitive occupants poking their heads out. Outside one of the stalls, I see Grace. A vet, whom I've seen many times at the farm, is inside the stall with a mare named Princess who is lying down and neighing loudly. I watch in wonderment as Princess gives birth. The vet yells,

'It's a female!' and he clears the mucus from the filly's mouth as Princess turns to lick her. Before too long the little foal is standing and drinking milk."

Gwen continues, "I still remember Marty's words, 'Well. that was a good night's work. Let's go up to the house; Grace and I have a surprise for you.' "

Looking at the picture in Gwen's hand again, I remark "That must have been so thrilling!"

"Yes, that's the most exciting moment of my life," Gwen replies and continues with her story.

"Grace then cuts me a big piece of cake and gives me a glass of milk. Marty pours out some coffee for himself and Grace, and we all settle around the table. It's then that Marty breaks the most wonderful news I've ever heard! This scene is etched in my brain. Marty begins 'You've been working around here for free since you were a wee one about this high, and he holds his hand about a meter off the ground. Well, Grace and I have talked, and we've decided that we want to give you Princess's foal. You can keep her here, so it won't cost you anything.' "

Gwen beams as she continued her story. "I couldn't believe my ears. I fly out of my chair and embrace and kiss Marty and Grace with tears in my eyes. Marty asks me what I'm going to name her. I think a while and then say Rose; I'm going to call her Rose. Marty says that Rose is a very pretty name, but asks, 'Why Rose?' I reply that Dad always gives roses to Mom to show her how much he loves her, so I call her Rose to show how much I love her and you guys."

Gwen gives her picture of Rose a kiss before she continues, "Marty first gives me riding lessons on one of his *old school masters*, as he calls the horse he uses to teach me. Marty rode dressage in the Olympics for England before he came to Canada. When Rose turns four I get to sit on her for the first time. I can feel how much we trust each other from the very beginning. Well, Marty has been my coach ever since; in fact, he's here coaching me. I'm so lucky."

I then relay to Gwen my experiences with Skotch and how fortunate I am to have him. As we hug, I know that our common love of horses will make us life-long friends, real soul mates.

The next day is the team competition for Skotch and me. We go through our usual routine of getting ready. As we enter the warm-up ring, all the dust the myriad of horses creates makes me cough. I then spot Gwen on Rose; Gwen is doing bending work to get Rose supple. I can see her coach, who must be Marty, giving her instructions and encouragement as she and Rose ride by him. Alana meets me, and we start our work. Skotch is on his best behavior, but the realization of how big this competition is really hits me.

When it's time to go to the show ring, my stomach is tied in a knot. On my way to the ring, I feel nauseous and must dismount and run to the bushes and throw up. I'm so ashamed. Vomiting leaves me feeling weak, but I must go on. Alana hands me a tissue to clean my mouth before I remount. With a very worried look on his face, Dad asks if I can continue, but I can't let Gwen and the rest of the team down.

As I ride down the center line for my test, I can feel that my terror is being transmitted down to Skotch. About half way through our test, I start to relax a bit, which is reflected in Skotch's movements. By the end of the test, Skotch and I are really performing up to our potential, but it's too late to get a good overall score. I feel so sorry for Gwen and our team mates. What's is sad is that Gwen and Rose must have been brilliant because they obtain one of the best scores of the competition. In the end, our team finishes sixth, out of the ribbons. The Ontario team is second, just behind one of the American teams. When I see Gwen later, I'm at a loss for words. I feel so sorry I let everyone down. Gwen gives me a hug and says not to worry about it. She tells me that she froze during the first time she competed at a Young Riders' Championship and completely forgot the test, so she couldn't even finish.

She says, "Let's go have some ice cream and forget all about the competition. Everything looks better after ice cream."

I conclude Gwen is a true soul mate. By the time we finish our treat, Gwen even has me laughing.

The next day is the individual rider competition. Both June and Gwen have qualified, so Penny and I are in the bleachers watching and cheering them on. Gwen and Rose look fantastic when they enter the show area. I notice that the judges look up and take notice as soon as they see them, which is a very good sign. Gwen has Rose very supple with her weight carried completely on her back legs. Their bending work is a thing of beauty. Rose's extended trot draws *Aahs* from the crowd. Her flying changes are perfect, and Rose keeps an active canter behind when they perform their pirouette turns. Their performance is breathtaking! Both Penny and I cheer as loud as we can.

Then it's June's and Champion's turn. They look magnificent and regal. Their performance is as impressive as Gwen's and Rose's, but perhaps a bit more elegant. When the scores are posted, June places first and Gwen is third. I am so proud of my friends. That evening June, Penny, Gwen and I along with our families and coaches go out to dinner. We all have a festive time recalling our adventures and laughing with each other. For me, the highlight of the competition is the wonderful friendships I have formed. I'm so happy for June and Gwen when I see the Canadian flags raised and hear the Canadian national anthem played. I vow that Skotch and I will return next year, and, who knows, we might even have the

Canadian flag raised for us. Little do I know at the time that events would hijack that dream, but lead Skotch and me into a whole new adventure!

A couple of months after I return from the Young Riders' Championship, I receive a jolt. Alana comes into the stable where I'm grooming Skotch. I put down my brush to greet her, but with a serious look on her face Alana says,

"Lauren, I have some news that may be disturbing to you. Gustave and I are returning to Germany. Gustave has an opportunity to work at the stable of one of the Grand Masters of dressage, Mark Schuller. I can train with his wife Helga, who is also a Grand Prix Rider."

"Oh," I respond, as disappointment wells up inside me.

"But the good news is that if your parents give their permission, you and Skotch can come with us. You can stay with us and work at the stable to pay for Skotch's board. This is the chance of a lifetime for you and Skotch! What do you say?"

I reply with a stunned look on my face, "Well, I don't know. I'm not sure my folks will let me. I don't know if they can afford it." As I suspected, my folks are hesitant to let me go to Germany since I am only 16. When I tell them that I can stay with Gustave and Alana, Mom and Dad are at least willing to think about it. However, when they find out the unbelievable cost involved in shipping Skotch by air, they are obliged to say it's impossible.

Later that week, Mrs. Grayson comes into the tack room as I'm cleaning Skotch's bridle. She comes over and puts her hand on my shoulder,

"What's the matter dear, you look so glum."

I don't mean it to happen, but all my unhappiness and tears come pouring out. I then blurt out,

"Gustave and Alana are going back to Germany, and I have no one to help me with Skotch. I'm afraid that if I try to ride him on my own, I'll ruin him."

"Why, don't you go with them?" asks Mrs. Grayson.

"I want to, but my folks don't have the money to send Skotch and me."

Mrs. Grayson takes her hand off my shoulder and rubs her chin for a while. Then she says,

"You know Lauren, you so resemble me that you are like the daughter I never had. I admire how much you love the horses. Therefore, if it is alright with your folks, I'll pay for you and Skotch to go to Germany.

I leap to my feet and hug and kiss her. But then I pull away.

"We can never pay you back."

"Don't worry dear, you just did, with your kiss and hug."

I think, *So I am going to Germany! Skotch is going back to the land of his birth! I can't believe it.*

Shakespeare: *Just as we finish Chapter 2, it turns 5:00 PM (Vince taught me how to tell time). Lauren looks worn out. I'm feeling peckish and ready for my food and walk. Even Vince looks tired. He tells me that remembering Lauren's competitions is exhausting, since he always feels like he's riding every step with her. So, we all agree to call it quits for the day and start again tomorrow.*

Shakespeare: *The next day as we assemble once again, I feel envious of Skotch. I've always wanted to visit the home of my ancestry, Scotland. I wonder what it was like for my forbearers herding sheep over the moors. I asked Skotch how much he remembered of Germany. He told me that the farm where he was raised was much smaller than where he is now. Also, he did not like the trip over. He first remembers being taken in a trailer to a place where these big flying birds were. He was then led into a stall that moved and loaded into one of these huge flying beasts. He couldn't see what was happening, but suddenly his portable stall lurched up at an angle for quite a while, and his ears started to hurt. It got a little better later on when things leveled out. But then the whole process repeated when he descended. It was all quite unnerving. The only pleasant memory he had was after he landed, and a nice lady patted him on the nose and gave him carrots. After another long trailer ride, he came to his current place, where the nice lady greeted him again with more carrots. Skotch said that if it was up to him he would stay put at his current place. He was happy to just leave memories of his homeland in the past. I sympathize with his view point, but I can also see why Lauren wanted to get such outstanding training. However, if Lauren had known at the time how Skotch felt, I'm pretty sure she wouldn't have taken him to Germany. I didn't share Skotch's feelings about travelling from Germany with Lauren because I didn't want to make her feel bad. Lauren arrives after breakfast, and we begin our story again.*

Chapter Three: Germany

THE FIRST STEP IN GOING to Germany is a trip to their Embassy in Toronto to apply for a visa. In addition, Skotch must be isolated for several weeks. To meet all the requirements, Skotch is quarantined in a stall away from other horses, and we have to put up screening to prevent insects from biting him. Mrs. Grayson provides a stall in an old unused barn, and Dad buys and installs the screening. He also arranges all the necessary paperwork and vet inspections. At the end of three weeks, my visa and all preparations are complete. A man with a horse trailer arrives,.and we're off!

Arriving at the Toronto airport, we go to the cargo area. It takes some searching, but we finally find the correct place. The horse trailer is backed into position, and Skotch is off loaded. After a final vet check, I lead Skotch into a stall on wheels. The airport personnel explain that they can't take a chance on a horse getting loose on the runway. If he did, they would have to shoot him. The thought makes me shudder. Since I'm going as a groom for Skotch and several other horses, I can stay with Skotch in a little room that is part of the portable stall. We are towed out to the plane where a big crane lifts the whole stall into a special compartment of the plane. All the horses and I are in a part of the plane located behind the passengers. With us are dogs and cats in their cages. We all must remain in our compartment for a couple of hours until the baggage is loaded and the passengers board. Even though I have a seat with the passengers reserved for me, I stay with Skotch to be sure he's okay. When the plane takes off, I feed the horses carrots, so their chewing will keep their ears from hurting. It's amazing how many people that I tell about this experience are surprised that Skotch isn't drugged. My answer is, "How would you like to travel with a 700 kilogram[28] drunk!"

During the flight, a stewardess asks if she can bring back some children to see the horses. I tell her it's okay. It is really enjoyable to look at the amazed expression on their faces when they see how big Skotch is. I let the braver ones give Skotch a carrot to munch on. The delight in the children's eyes and their squeals are wonderful!

After we land in Germany, I go through a myriad of paperwork. Luckily, Dad has arranged for a broker to help guide me through all the forms and for Skotch and me to be transported to the stable. Alana and Gustave are there to greet us. After Skotch is settled in a stall, Gustave takes me to meet Herr Schuller, which is what everyone calls him. After greeting me in broken English, he hands me a spade and, motioning to his garden, tells me in German, which Gustave translates, that I'm to start weeding. Apparently, it's a tradition that anyone coming to see the Riding Master for the first time is expected to spend a good amount of time working in his garden. Later Alana tells me that this rule even applied to Gustave and her. Apparently, Gustave still has calluses on his hands from his gardening detail. When I think of Gustave, who is so dignified, stooping to do gardening, it makes me chuckle. Even though the flight and time change left me exhausted, I labor for several hours digging out weeds. Finally, Alana says that I can quit and accompany them to the apartment Gustave has rented for us.

[28] One kilogram is 2.2 pounds.

When I come down for breakfast the next morning, the sun is just beginning to rise and Alana is making coffee.

"Where's Gustave?" I enquire.

"Oh, he's out getting bread."

I later learn that Germans take great pride in the fact that they don't put preservatives in any of their food or drinks, so everything is bought fresh and only kept for a few days at most. Breakfast consists of bread, cold meats and coffee. I have to get used to not having juice, fruit or cereal. After we eat, Alana, Gustave, and I are off to work. When we arrive, I begin right away. The other girls at the stable are very nice and get me started cleaning all the tack while they feed the horses and groom them. Just as they finish, Herr Schuller comes in and immediately gets the most terrified look on his face. He screams something in German as he runs to the exit!

The other grooms then translate his words as "Spiders! Spiders! Get them down. Kill them immediately," So all we grooms have to stop everything we are doing, get brooms, and sweep down the few cobwebs that have formed. Herr Schuller does not reappear until he is assured that the stable is spider free, and he will be safe. I observe that despite Herr Schuller occasional crazy behavior, he is indeed a master when it comes to riding. In addition, even though years of riding have taken a toll on his body, which causes him to walk slightly bent over and with a bit of a limp, when he mounts a horse it is pure magic. He can take any horse in the barn, regardless of the quality, and make them look like a champion. I have come to understand why people put up with his quirks.

Another trait of Herr Schuller that I admire is that the horses always come first. The other grooms told me about a time when a wealthy client, who was boarding a horse at Herr Schuller's stable, was told by Herr Schuller not to compete his horse at an upcoming show because the horse was lame. The client competed his horse anyway. The next day Herr Schuller took all this client's possessions and tack and piled them outside the gate to his property. He then took the client's horse and tied him up to the gate and telephoned the disobedient client to collect his belongings. Two lessons are obvious from this story. First Herr Schuller will not stand for any abuse of horses and second, no one crosses Herr Schuller. For the first month Alana teaches Skotch and me, but I then notice that Helga starts watching my lessons.

One day as I'm warming up Skotch in the ring, Helga comes out and tells me she will give the lesson. She said that she has spoken to Alana about it. Helga starts by instructing Skotch and me with basic riding skills, which greatly improves my ability to really bend Skotch around my leg. I can feel that this bending work is enabling Skotch to carry more of his weight on his hind end. By the end of the lesson, Skotch feels very light in front, and he becomes very easy to ride. From then on Helga teaches me once or twice a week. I begin to feel stronger in my lower back and legs. I'm no longer *a mosquito with spurs* as Alana used to call me. The combination of Alana's and Helga's instruction complements each other to produces a drastic improvement in my riding.

The next week is Gustave's birthday, so he takes Alana, Helga, Herr Schuller and me out to a restaurant. This is a real lesson on how different customs are in Germany. When we enter the restaurant, Gustave goes to every table and greets everyone. At first, I'm embarrassed, but everyone reacts as if this behavior is perfectly normal. I don't drink alcohol, but a lot of Schnapps is consumed by everyone else. After quite a few drinks, Herr Schuller laments, "I don't have any real Germans working for me." At the time, I don't understand what he's talking about since he has many grooms from the Würzburg area in his employ.

When I ask Alana about it later, she explains that Herr Schuller is from the Hannover area and many people from Herr Schuller's generation don't consider southern Germans real Germans. They think that Bavarians, which he calls them, just want to party all the time and are not serious enough. In turn, the southern Germans think people from the north are too formal and don't know how to have a good time. I never realized that Germans have the same kind of divisiveness I hear about in the northern and southern United States. Even in Canada there tends to be a rift between easterners and westerners. I decide that this problem is universal.

When it comes time to pay, I start to take out my purse, but I'm informed by Alana that, in Germany, the birthday person pays all his guests' bills. When we get home, Gustave wants to watch television, so Alana makes some popcorn. When I put my first handful in my mouth, I'm so surprised, I almost spit it out. In Germany, they put sugar instead of salt on their popcorn! I indeed have a lot to learn.

For a while all goes very well, that is, until Skotch's mouth and curiosity get me in trouble again. Entering the stable one morning, I see that the water faucet is turned on, and all the stalls are flooded. In addition, all the horses' blankets have been taken off their stall doors and thrown around on the floor. There's no question as to whom is to blame, since Skotch's stall door is the only one that's open. I think, *Thank goodness Herr Schuller and Helga are away from the stable at a show for a few days, or I might have had a premature departure for home.* Thus, I must clean up all of Skotch's mess in addition to my other chores. What really gets me mad is that while I'm busy mopping up the water, replacing all the wet straw, and hanging all the blankets out to dry, Skotch goes into his stall and is snoring after his all-night party, but it's impossible for me to stay angry at him, particularly when he later shows me he is sorry by nuzzling me.

When Helga and Herr Schuler return to the stable, Herr Schuler takes an interest in Skotch and me, and, much to my amazement, even gives me a few lessons, with Alana translating the German to

English. I guess Helga must have peaked his curiosity about my riding. I'm even more awed when Helga asks me if I would like to go to the next show with them as her groom and show Skotch. Her question is so surprising that I just stand there gawking, but I finally gather my senses enough to agree. When I tell Alana and Gustave, I feel that they are not only caught off guard but are a little jealous since their words of congratulations ring a little hollow. After all, Gustave has not even been invited to go to a show with Helga and Herr Schuller yet. I later find out from the other grooms, who overheard Helga and Herr Schuller talking, that Helga said she really likes the way that I love and take extra special care of the horses. I see that all my true regard for horses has paid off.

On the day of the show, I must get up extra early to prepare not only Skotch, but also Helga's horse. He's an elegant mover named Prince Gregory. I'm also tasked with helping pack the horse van, which has room for up to six horses, plus all the trunks containing their gear. It's quite a production and reminds me of stories I read in school about kings taking a whole entourage with them when they travel. I ride with Helga in her Mercedes, which follows the van. To get to the show grounds we travel along some narrow country roads. At one point, we meet a truck travelling in the opposite direction. I think, *There's no way we can possibly pass.* But somehow Herr Schuller manages to inch the van past the truck though a little paint does get scraped off both the van and the truck. Herr Schuller thus shows his prowess at driving is as great as his riding ability. Helga says that such occurrences are common in Germany due to the narrowness of the rural roads. When we arrive at the show grounds, the packing process I underwent in the morning is reversed.

While I go for some water for the horses, I can't believe what I see – it's Gwen! She drops her bucket and runs over to me. We hug and both start to talk at once. We laugh, and I ask,

"What are you doing here? I didn't know you were in Germany."

"Yes, after you left for Germany, Marty arranged for me to take Rose and go to Herr Albert's stable to train and work."

"Doesn't Herr Albert own the most famous stallion in the world, King Schultz? I'm sure I overheard Helga talk about him with some clients."

"Yes, he does. It's quite nerve racking when I take care of him knowing I have been entrusted with a horse worth more than a million dollars!"

With that revelation, my jaw drops. "You really get to take care of the best stallion in the world!"

"Yes, isn't it nuts?"

"What's he like? I would love to see him."

"You should come to the stable. It's not too far away from where you're located."

We agree we will get together, but we then hurry back to our jobs.

After returning with my bucket of water, I spot Helga sitting in a lawn chair and ask her about the possibility of going to visit Gwen and seeing King Schultz. Helga looks quite shocked at my request.

"My dear, I know it is different in North America, but here it would be considered very rude for a visitor to just show up at a stable. You would be summarily escorted off the grounds and told to never return. You must seek permission and be invited as a guest. But it so happens that Riding Master Herr Albert is a good friend of mine, and I'm planning on going over to his stable for some business anyway. I'll ask him if you can come along. I'm positive he won't mind. Be sure to complement him on his horses, especially King Schultz; he is quite vain about them. Now, don't you have some work to do?"

I just want to hug her, but restrain myself, since I sense it would be a breach of etiquette.

When it's time for the competition to begin, I groom and braid Helga's horse for her. I then lead him out to the warm-up ring for Helga to mount. Herr Schuller is at his post, seated by the ring, and is barking out orders for his students. Herr Schuller doesn't bother competing anymore since he already has achieved the rank of Riding Master and has nothing more to prove. After the warm up, Helga and her Grand Prix[29] horse look elegant as they enter the show ring. Her test is a work of art as she and her horse seem to float around the ring while performing their movements. Her elegant performance earns her a third place.

Later, it's my turn to compete. As I ride Skotch into the practice ring, Herr Schuller nods for me to begin my warm up. By now I have learned enough German to figure out what he wants. He has me do a lot of bending work so Skotch becomes supple. Helga had previously decided that I should only enter a basic class, since the competition would be of a whole different magnitude compared with Canada. As I go through the test, I can feel the difference Helga's and Herr Schuller's coaching has made. Skotch's performance is magnificent, and I'm quite pleased. Helga even gives a smile of approval. Much to my astonishment, Skotch and I finish third, which is amazing considering there were over fifty riders in the class!

The next week Helga is true to her word and invites me to go with her to Herr Albert's horse farm. While Helga meets with Herr Albert, I'm free to find Gwen. I'm so excited that when I find her I run up and hug her. We both jump up and down and squeal. We then sit down and talk until our jaws hurt. We arrange that we will take a trip together. I've always wanted the visit the historic village of Rothenburg ob der Tauber, so we settle on that as a destination.

---

[29] Grand Prix is the highest level of competitive dressage riding.

I tell Gwen, "It's so wonderful to hear and speak English. I've learned enough German to make myself understood, but communication is a long slow process"

Gwen laughs and nods in agreement. After a while, Helga and Herr Albert appear. Helga says,

"I explained to Herr Albert that you would like to see King Schultz, and he has consented. He says Gwen can get him out of his stall for us."

When everyone arrives at King Schultz's stall, my mouth drops. He is so magnificent. His shoulders are higher than my head, and his coat is a glimmering black with a white blaze on his forehead. When Penny leads him from his stall, his high-stepping movement and the power in his stride are beyond what I thought possible. In addition to his amazing physical attributes, I note he has the kindest eyes I have ever seen in a horse. I try to express my wonderment and gratitude for having the privilege of seeing this god-like Pegasus in the best German I can muster. Herr Albert smiles and nods at my attempt. On our way home from the stable, Helga grins as I rave about King Schultz. She tells me that she went to see Herr Albert to get his approval for several of her mares that are in season to breed to King Schultz. Helga explains that Herr Albert will only consent to having the finest mares bred by his stallion. I can't imagine how much the stud fees are, probably tens of thousands of dollars.

The attention I'm receiving from Helga and Herr Schuller causes a bit of tension between Gustave and Alana and myself. The fact that Gustave and Alana often fight among themselves adds to the stress I feel. My folks never fight, at least not in front of me. The tension is relieved a bit when Helga tells Gustave and Alana that they can come to the next show with Herr Schuller and her, but I decide that I should move to Herr Schuller's farm and stay in an apartment above the horses with the rest of the grooms. With my broken German and the grooms' meager English, everyone manages to overcome the language barrier. The other grooms are all very curious about life in Canada. When I tell them about the vastness and beauty of the country, they all want to visit someday. Being friends helps all of us with the ardors of the job, which involves starting before 5:30 AM and not finishing sometimes till 8:00PM. One aspect of working at the stable I'm not prepared for is how the clients at the stable view me. One day I'm cleaning a bridle for Helga, when a middle-aged client named Madam Maria Holtz comes into the tack room,

"Oh dear, would you please clean my boots for me. I'm afraid I landed in a mud puddle when I dismounted. Oh, and could you please open a window, it's terribly stuffy in here."

With that she plops into a chair and sips her iced drink. I don't know what to do since my position doesn't include waiting on clients. Also, coming from Canada, I'm not accustomed to being treated as a servant. However, I don't want to offend her because she's a very rich and important client of Helga's and Herr Schuller. So, I bite my lip and obey the commands.

To top everything off, when Madam Holtz finishes her drink, she says in a dismissive manner, "I must go now, so just put my boots in my locker after you finish with them."

How I want to throw her boots at her and tell her off, but I just bite my lip harder and restrain my impulses. This episode repeats itself several times. I'm about ready to tell Helga that no matter who Madam Holtz is, I'm not going to put up with her, but then to my amazement Madam Holtz issues me an invitation,

"Dear, you've been so kind and have treated my horses so well, I would like to give you a little treat. How would you like to accompany me to Würzburg? I'll talk to Helga and get you some time off."

Before I can say a word, Madam Holtz says, "Good, that's all settled," and she's gone. I'm left with my mouth wide open. A week later Maria, as she now insists I call her, is as good as her word. Maria drives me on the autobahn into Würzburg in her Mercedes. The first thing we do when we arrive is go to a ladies clothing store. Here Maria tries on and buys several very expensive dresses. Then, to my amazement, Maria insists that I try on some clothes. I find a sweater and two slacks that I like. Before I can say a word, Maria takes out a wad of bills and pays for them in cash. She then asks if I need any riding things.

"I do need a new pair of riding pants," I utter in a quiet, hesitant voice.

"Done," Maria says and whisks me off to a store specializing in riding clothes.

After our shopping trip, Maria treats me to lunch and a fancy dessert.

"We have to celebrate our purchases," Maria exclaims.

As we ride home, I muse how different things are here in Germany. I was never asked to wait on a client when I worked at stables in Canada, but then, no Canadian client ever rewarded me for helping them and taking care of their horse. I now understand that Maria feels her requests are justified and appropriate given my social rank here in Germany. I also see that Maria admires my love and care for the horses. I think, *People are sure complicated and hard to judge. I'm so grateful to Skotch for giving me the opportunity to come to Germany and broaden my perspective on life.*

At the next horse show it's agreed that Skotch and I have progressed enough that I should show in a medium class. It's another big show that is attended by many prominent German dressage riders. The show goes well, and Skotch and I place fifth. To my mind, at least some of the horses who place ahead of us didn't perform any better than Skotch and me. When I mention this to Alana, she explains that both the horses and riders who placed ahead of us are well known to the judges. I guess the judging is more subjective and political than I thought.

After the competition, the organizers of the show are putting on a big riding exhibition. All the horses from Herr Schuller's stable have been sent home in the early afternoon, except Skotch, because we competed late in the competition. One of the other grooms is going to come back for Skotch and me with a small horse trailer after the demonstration. I'm happy since it means that I can see the exhibition. I sit with Helga and Herr Schuller. As soon as the riding starts, even I can see that the performances the organizers arranged are anything but excellent. German riding spectators are quite knowledgeable and critical and are becoming very restless. As the exhibition continues I even hear a few boos starting. Just then one of the organizers comes running over to where Herr Schuller and the rest of us are sitting. By now I've learned enough German to know what they are saying.

"Herr Schuller, Can you please ride and save our exhibition? If you don't, our reputation will be ruined."

"I would be happy to, but I have no riding clothes and no horse. All our horses are back at my horse farm."

"We can provide a riding outfit for you," says the organizer in a pleading voice while motioning to another organizer who is running towards us with riding apparel in his hand."

"But I have no horse," replies Herr Schuller.

"You can ride Skotch. He's still here. His mane is even still braided," I manage to blurt out in broken German.

"Oh yes, I forgot. Well, go get him ready," orders Herr Schuller.

So, off I go to give Skotch a quick brushing, put on his saddle and reins, and bring him to the area where Herr Schuller is waiting in a riding jacket that he has managed to squeeze into, despite it being too small. His pants seem to fit him okay and fortunately he has a habit of always bring along his riding boots. His top hat barely fits him. I have to control my impulse to laugh out loud. He warms Skotch up behind the arena while an announcement is made that Riding Master Schuller is going to give a riding demonstration. The crowd quiets down in anticipation. Herr Schuller and Skotch enter; Skotch trots to the center of the ring and makes a perfect halt. Absolute silence descends over the area. Then the music starts, and the performance begins. Herr Schuller has Skotch trot down the center line, turn, and then cross the diagonal in an extended trot. Skotch just seems to fly across the ring with his legs flashing out in full extension. The crowd emits *Ahhs* in admiration. Herr Schuller then collects him back and crosses the other diagonal doing flying changes every stride. Skotch resembles a school boy skipping down the street in perfect harmony with the tune that is playing in the background. Skotch and Herr Schuller are now drawing wild yells and whistles of approval, but they are not done. Herr Schuller then takes Skotch down the center line doing a passage movement[30]. With that the crowd claps with a thunderous roar in time with every one of Skotch's steps. I can't believe my eyes. I've never seen such animation and power in a passage before. It is as if Herr Schuller's and Skotch's body have become one, and Skotch is completely given over to Herr Schuller's will. As Skotch continues his passage, Herr Schuller lets go of the reins with one hand and waves to the crowd with this top hat while Skotch still continues his passage with as much vigor as before. The crowd goes wild, and the beat of their applause and stamping of their feet to Skotch's footfalls is deafening. Herr Schuller finishes his performance with a perfect piaffe pirouette[31] in the middle of the ring. With that the crowd

---

[30] A slow elevated trot with maximum collection. A Grand Prix movement.

[31] An elevated trot on the spot while the horse is rotating 360°.

becomes crazy with cheering and shouting. Everyone around me wants to know, who is this marvelous horse? Skotch has achieved superstar status! The next day a picture of Herr Schuller and Skotch is in all the papers that are delivered to the stable. Also, the staff at Herr Schuller's horse farm are busy shooing reporters and photographers away, so everyone can keep up their routine. I get offers to buy Skotch for hundreds of thousands of dollars. Of course, I refuse each one no matter how much they offer. Selling Skotch would be like selling a child of mine. All the fame doesn't seem to have any effect on Skotch, who is only interested in getting his grain and treats of carrots and apples.

Finally, the day comes for Gwen and me to take our trip. I've been looking forward to getting away from the hectic schedule of the stable. We meet at the train station and run to the train to make sure we aren't late. After checking with the conductor to be sure we're on the right train, we settle in seats in the second-class carriage and have a great gab fest until we arrive at our destination. From the train station, we walk up the hill through the modern section of Rothenburg ob der Tauber to the old town, which is surrounded by a huge stone wall. We enter through fortified archways into a scene from a mystic tale. I half expect to see gnomes and hobbits roaming around, but the streets are only filled with tourists like us. The lane way is lined with half-timbered housed that are decorated with window boxes containing red geraniums. Other houses have step gables or "S" shaped gables in the form of dragons. At the end of the street is a tall, stone clock tower with an archway at its base through which we continue walking in wonderment until we arrived at the center of the village.

Here we listen in as a tour guide describes all the sights. He starts off by describing the town hall or Rathhaus that is made of brown stone. At its base, it has a series of arches, and a tower rises out of its center. It also has many little dormer windows sticking out from its roof. Behind it is a pinkish building that has an even higher tower. It is clear to me that the builders of this time sure love towers because you can see them rising up from all over the city. Just as we are about to move on, a clock on another building rings one o'clock, and two windows open, revealing two mechanical men in medieval dress. The one on our right starts drinking from a giant tankard. A nearby guide explains to his group that the one on the left is a general called Tilly. He conquered the city and is going to destroy it unless someone can drink all the wine in a giant tankard in one gulp. According to the guide, the tankard holds three and one-half liters. The man on the right, named Nusch, is glad to oblige and drains the tankard in one go, thus saving the city. The guide finishes his tale by saying that afterwards, while everyone celebrates their deliverance, Nusch sleeps for three days! This story sounds far-fetched, but everyone seems to accept it in good fun.

We then walk on and notice the shops all have wrought-iron signs hanging in front to indicate what kind of business it is. When I see one of the signs, I can't believe my eyes. There, in the best middle age tradition, is a small hanging metal sign showing the arches of McDonalds. After our initial shock, Gwen and I both nod in agreement and rush in to order a hamburger, fries, and a Coke. We both agree that it is wonderful to have a taste of home. After lunch, we get down to the really serious business of shopping. It's so much fun going through all the shops. I end up buying a small ornate putter mug and pitcher set. It seems like an appropriate souvenir. Gwen buys a small statue of a knight on a horse. We both laugh at how touristy we are. One shop in particular stands out. It brags that every day is Christmas there. They sell everything concerning Christmas every day except, ironically, Christmas day. One item that particularly catches my eye is a giant rotating hand carved wooden toy that contains many tiers with small statues on each tier depicting winter Christmas scenes. I have a hard time taking my eyes off of it. Neither Gwen nor I can afford the giant toy, but both of us buy a much smaller, simpler version of it. We both comment that our purchases will be just perfect for the holidays.

As night approaches, we bid a hesitant farewell to Rothenburg and board the train for home. We're so tired after our excursion, we both sleep all the way. Fortunately, a kind gentlemen who overheard us talking about where we had to get off, wakes us when we reach our stop. It's lucky he was sitting by us, or we might have missed our stop and woke up in Hamburg, the train's ultimate destination. I put my purchases by my bed when I arrive home as a reminder of my wonderful day.

As wonderful as my time away was, Skotch and I are overjoyed to see each other the next morning. After finishing my chores, I spend the rest of my time grazing Skotch and offering him treats. He reciprocates by nuzzling me. Helga and Herr Schuller now take over almost all of my lessons. My riding skills are improving dramatically. After several months, I'm shocked when Helga tells me that Skotch and I should ride at the dressage competition at Aachen, Germany. Helga says she has discussed this matter with Herr Schuller, and he agrees. This is an FEI international show, so the lowest level I can compete in is Prix St. Georges[32]. Skotch and I work hard preparing for the show. Alana and Gustave are also coming and Gustave is competing at the Grand Prix level. As we all enter the show grounds, we see thousands of horse trailers. Only the Olympics are a bigger dressage competition in Germany than this one at Aachen. This competition is not just for dressage, but also for stadium jumping, driving of carts, and three-day

[32] The lowest FEI test. It is the same level as ridden at the Pan Am games.

eventing[33], so it involves thousands of the world's best horses. I first help settle the horses from our stable in their stalls and then check the competition schedule. I compete first on day two. Thankfully I had competed in the Young Riders' Championship, because it gives me a glimpse of what to expect, although this competition is in a much higher league. Fortunately, Skotch and all the other horses from Herr Schuller's stable pass the vet check. This time I'm especially careful that Skotch doesn't grab my watch band.

On the day of my test, Herr Schuller works with Skotch and me during our warmup, so Skotch is at his peak when we go to the competition area. It seems to me that Skotch's reputation after Herr Schuller's ride on him precedes us, since we have the attention of all five judges as soon as we enter and trot around the area surrounding the competition ring. I think, *No pressure, Ha ha.* Again I'm glad for all the previous high pressure situations Skotch and I have endured. They steeled us. After the bell rings, I have Skotch canter into the ring and halt. It is completely silent, as if the audience is anticipating something exceptional. I really push Skotch's hind end, so he has a perfect, square stop. At my command, Skotch then starts to trot and goes into some bending work. All the training I have done with Helga and Herr Schuller really pays off since Skotch is so supple and responsive to my legs. Skotch then starts an extended trot. I can feel the power of the locomotive between my legs, and we fly across the ring with Skotch's front legs shooting out in front. He then comes right back to me in a collected trot. The feeling is breath taking. It's pure poetry in motion. Skotch then starts the bending work in the opposite direction. As he bends around my leg, his ears perk up in

---

33 A competition in which the horse must compete in dressage, cross country jumping and stadium jumping.

attentiveness. Skotch then starts the collected walk and does perfect half pirouettes in both the right and left direction. I strain my back muscles to keep his hind legs moving in an active manner. Uninformed bystanders might think that the walk is the easiest gait, but, in fact, during this gait the rider must work the hardest. Skotch then takes up the canter and does his bending work. I next have Skotch perform half-pirouettes at canter. I call on my legs to keep him turning and my back muscles to keep his hind legs active but not hopping while he turns in a tight circle. I pray I will be strong enough; Skotch does the movement perfectly. All the long hours of riding on Skotch and other horses have developed my back muscles, so I can ride the test in a proper manner. All we have left are the flying changes, first every fourth stride on one diagonal and then every third stride down the other diagonal. Going into this movement I realize we actually have a chance to get a ribbon. I pray the pressure doesn't get to me. As we turn and face the first diagonal, all my training comes to the fore, and I go into auto-pilot. The fours go perfect, now the threes. Skotch has done them many times at home, but can he do them now when everything is at stake? We start down the line, and my leg swings back indicating the first flying change, which is then followed by two canter strides. The second, third and fourth sets of flying changes are fine, but on the fifth, Skotch gets excited and almost changes after the second instead of the third stride. Fortunately, I'm able to compensate, and he does them correctly. I wonder, *Did the judges notice how he almost got it wrong? Of course they have; these are international judges, and all five of them have eyes like eagles.* I manage to gather my senses, and we finish the test with a perfect, square halt. As we leave the ring, the crowd gives an appreciative applause. I'm haunted by the thought, *Did we do enough?* When we exit the ring, Alana and Gustave congratulate me. They seem to have gotten over their jealousy. They both exclaim that this is the best they have ever seen me ride and that Skotch's gaits and changes were of championship caliber. Helga says she is very proud of both Skotch and me. Even Herr Schuller gives us one of his rare smiles and nods approval. As I lead Skotch back to the stable to groom him, I keep asking myself, *How will we stack up against the other competitors?*

Later, as I'm brushing Skotch and giving him lots of treats, Alana comes running into the stable and yells,

"Lauren you did it! You and Skotch did it!"

"Did what?" I ask. "Did we place in the top ten?"

"The top ten. You and Skotch won the competition. You are Prix St. Georges champions at Aachen!" I just stand there in disbelief. Later, as I put Skotch's saddle on him and ride out to the awards ceremony, it all seems like a dream. I can't take it all in. When they hand me the first-place ribbon and wrap a champion's blanket around Skotch, I can't help but start crying tears of joy. I think of Zing and feel her loving presence with us. Skotch and I then take a victory lap around the arena. We float around the ring as on a cloud. Then it's over, and I'm left with facing all the press; it's overwhelming. I'm showered with questions from reporters, *How did a riding combination from Canada beat all the best from England and Europe? Where am I going to compete next? When am I moving up to the grand prix? Am I going to breed my horse?*
The last question is easy since Skotch is a gelding and lacks the equipment to breed. I tell them that I'm proud to come from Canada and that Skotch and I achieved what we did because of all the wonderful people who helped us, most of all my parents and the best coaches ever. About the future, I can only shrug my shoulders and say I'm not sure what is next for us. Little do I know that our fate is going to be determined in such an unexpected manner.

Shakespeare: *After I finish typing, Vince immediately asks me, "What did Skotch think of this achievement? Was he excited, happy, proud?"*

I reply, "Skotch told me that he likes the attention he receives, in particular from Tender, but the only thing that really excites him are the apples and carrots he receives." When I explain to him how big an achievement winning at Aachen is, he says he's happy for Tender, but for him, it's just "another day at the office," and he grabs another mouthful of hay and starts chewing.

After finishing this chapter, I ask Lauren if she wants to continue tomorrow, but she indicates she just wants to press on to the end.

Chapter Four: Disaster and Home

AFTER WE GET BACK to Herr Schuller's farm, I decide to give Skotch the week off. I let him graze in the field and take him out on relaxing walking hacks. While on one of these hacks along a country road, the unthinkable happens. A jalopy full of kids races up behind us, and they start blasting their horn and laughing. Skotch begins to rear. The car then jets past us and emits black smoke with a load bang. One of the kids throws a can that hits Skotch. He keeps rearing, and despite my best efforts, Skotch finally bucks me off. The next thing I remember is seeing the car disappearing over a hill. In dread I think, *Where's Skotch? Where did he go?* Then the awful truth is revealed. He's thrashing about, tangled in some barb wire. I rush to him and pull at the wire to try to free him, but I can't, and inadvertently, he almost kicks me. I scream and holler until a farmer from a nearby house comes running. When he sees what happened, he returns to his house and comes back with some wire cutters. When Skotch gets up, he won't put any weight on one of his hind legs.

"No! No!" I scream. "This can't be happening." Finally gaining control of myself again, I have the farmer call Helga and tell her to bring a horse van and a vet. When they arrive, the vet gives Skotch a pain killer, so we can coax him onto the trailer with some carrots the farmer supplies. When we get him back to the stable yard, the vet cleans him up. He says that most of the scratches are superficial, but he's quite worried about one of Skotch's hind legs. He says to rest Skotch overnight, and he will examine his leg after the shot wears off.

I can't sleep all night and keep reliving the disastrous moment over and over in my mind. The next morning, I rush to Skotch's stall and see he won't put weight on his hind leg now that the drug has worn off. I'm waiting at the gate when the vet arrives. By injecting a local anesthetic to first Skotch's hoof area and then progressing up the leg, the vet confirms that the injury is in his leg, probably to a ligament since X-rays don't detect any broken bones.

The vet says in a solemn voice, "He will likely take a year of rest to recover. Even then I doubt you will ever be able to do dressage work with him again. I think you should retire him. He will be fine for pleasure riding, but not for hard dressage work."

That news is shattering and leaves me in tears.

Alana puts her arm around me and whispers, "I know this is hard, but thank God Skotch doesn't have to be put down."

After I recover from my initial shock, I have a serious decision to make. My German visa is about to expire, and I must decide whether or not to apply for a renewal. Even before Skotch's injury, I was thinking, I should go back home and continue my education. I remember Amy, the little girl with cerebral palsy I met after my riding demonstration. Thinking of her and how sweet she was, makes me think about becoming a nurse, so I can help kids like her. Helga and Herr Schuller invite me to stay and continue working for them, but I decide that it is time to go home. When I call my folks, they sound conflicted. They're happy I'm coming home, but sad that my success with Skotch is at an end. Dad and I must endure a bureaucratic nightmare once again to bring Skotch home, including the quarantine.

I'm so happy and relieved when we finally get back to Canada. In addition to my folks, Mrs. Grayson meets Skotch and me at the airport. She hugs me and exclaims how proud she is. When we arrive at the stable, I give Skotch lots of treats, and he nuzzles me and grabs onto my blouse with his lips. I think, *Same old Skotch. He's telling me how happy he is to be home with me!*

Two years later, I'm out in a field with Skotch. I've completed my high school and my first year in the nursing program and am on summer break. As predicted, my vet says that Skotch now is alright for pleasure riding, but not for hard work. I brought a newspaper in addition to a novel to read while Skotch grazes in the field by me. As I scan the paper, I notice an article about a local stable where children with all kinds of disabilities can come for riding therapy. The article describes that the owners of the stable are always looking for donations of suitable horses. My mind again goes to Amy, and how thrilled she was when she petted Skotch. He also seemed to enjoy her touch. Right then, I decide I will talk to the people operating the riding therapy program to see if Skotch is suitable. When I show them the vet report on Skotch and explain his situation, they agree to try him out to see if he's appropriate for their program. When Dad and I have Skotch trailered to the facility, all are very impressed by him. To test him, they do a mock ride in which one of the staff mounts him, and two other staff members hold onto leads from his halter. It seems to me that Skotch knows he's being tested and doesn't pull any *Skotchy* tricks. The head of the program is very pleased, and Skotch is accepted on the spot. I do have one request that the program leader accepts.

When I go home, I make a special phone call. When the time comes for Skotch's debut as a riding therapy horse, my folks plus some special guests, Amy and her parents, are present. When Amy sees Skotch, she wheels her chair right over to him and gives him a carrot that I had given her. The staff then put Amy up on the saddle, and her face just glows with happiness. As the staff leads Skotch around, I have never been so proud of him, not even when we won the Prix St. Georges at Aachen. I think back to all my wonderful experiences that would not have been possible without Skotch. Now he's going to continue to give such joy to all the children who ride him. As I watch him I think, He looks so regal. He definitely is, *Skotch The Magnificent!*

Shakespeare: *Though I have never ridden a horse, I wrote the following poem after communicating with Lauren. This poem must be read aloud in order to hear the rhythmic, pulsating beat of horse and rider as they execute various dressage moves.*

Skotch, The Magnificent

Steam--rising, engulfing both horse and rider.
Sun filters through hot sweat,
Collides with frigid, morning air.
Nostrils flaring, vapor blowing, muscles rippling,
He undulates up and down, up and down...
The trot, here on the spot. Right front, left hind –
Left front, right hind, again and again,
Elevation in complete synchrony, silent, relentless beats.
Ears... forward, listening, understanding;
The gaze... fixed, focused. The neck arched... a knight,
Outlined with white braids; muscles bulging, shining.
Hocks working, flexing, extending, with rhythmic precision.
The rider silent, seemingly still,
Yet guiding, urging with an unseen language.
Horse and rider, one in their happiness, one in their union.
This is beauty; this is harmony.
This is Dressage!

Tale Seven: Gray Wolf

Gray Wolf
(Photo credit by Glamstyle/Shutterstock)

Vince: *I'm startled one day when I go into my library and see Shakespeare pawing (literally) through my books. I enquire what he's looking for.*
Shakespeare: *What do you know about the Cree culture? I've become fascinated with how close they are to Nature and all the animals of the forest.*
Vince: *Well I know that there're a tribe of first nation's people that live in northern Ontario, but that's about the extent of my knowledge.*
Shakespeare: *That's about all I know also. I need to do some research on them for the last story in our book. Why don't you take me to the library and get me a card, so I can check out some books on the subject?*
Vince: *I don't think they give library cards to dogs. In fact, I remember a sign in the library that says no dogs are allowed.*

With that Shakespeare becomes irate. He growls and bites his mat like I have never seen him do before.
Shakespeare: *Don't these egregious cretins know who I am? I'm not just some cur off the street. What are they afraid of? Do they think I'm going to chew up their precious books?*
Vince: *I think that's exactly what they think.*
Shakespeare: *How dare they smear my good name with calumny!*
Vince: *Why don't you simply tell me what books you're looking for, and I'll go get them?*
Shakespeare: *I don't know what I'm looking for. I have to see it. You get me into that library, so I can select the appropriate books for myself!*
Vince: *I told you that the library doesn't let...*
Shakespeare: *Listen! I have an idea. Why don't you smuggle me into the library under your coat? That way I can select what I need.*
Vince: *Needless to say, I'm not too keen on this proposal, but finally, Shakespeare convinces me. It certainly is better than having him type nasty Emails to the library officials and getting me in trouble. So off we go. Fortunately, the library is pretty busy, hence none of the staff notices us. The section on the indigenous people is deserted, and Shakespeare can*

come out into the open and look at the books. I take the books down that I think are appropriate and show them to him; he either nods yes or no. In addition to books on the Cree language, surroundings, homes, diet and customs, he seems to be particularly interested in Cree legends about the forest spirits. After Shakespeare picks all the books he needs, he crawls back under my coat, and we go to the automatic checkout. Just as I finish checking out the last book, I hear a yell from the guard.

"Hey you, no dogs are allowed in here!"

I look back and see I have grown a tail out the back of my coat! Both Shakespeare and I run as fast as we can with the guard in fast pursuit. We finally managed to lose him, and we both give a huge sigh of relief. When we get home, Shakespeare pores over these book until late into the night. He labors on his story with such ardor, he refrains from eating or drinking. I'm very concerned for his health and am thinking of taking his computer away when he announces he's finished. When I read his tale, I'm certainly impressed. I love all his other writings, but I think this is his finest.

Gray Wolf

Forest spirits rage.
Mingan and Gray Wolf respond.
Together they win.

COME WITH ME BACK through time across the vast, shining waters called Kitchi-gami, north to the vast Boreal forest. Enter with me and smell the fresh scent from groves of black and white spruce, jack pine, balsam fir and white cedar. See the beauty of white birch trees shimmering against the dark forest. This vast wilderness rings with the sounds of a myriad of song birds. The skies are patrolled by great owls, hawks and eagles. The powerful black bears crash through the brush while the white-tailed deer spring over fallen, rotting logs, and hares hop looking for food, with their noses twitching, and try not to become food themselves. The elusive wild turkeys hide in the deep underbrush. The beavers gnaw at the trees and labor in constructing their lodges and dams. Taking advantage of the beavers' accomplishments, the mighty moose grazes on water plants near the banks of their pools.

Into this natural paradise come the Cree, who love this land and its creatures. They only take from the land what they need and what Nature can spare. They also acknowledge the woodland spirits, the ones who help and protect them, and the ones they dread. Into this world, a young baby first opens his eyes. The first people he sees are his mother Nadie and his father Kitchi. Nadie is often consulted by the other women of the tribe because of her wisdom and thus lives up to the meaning of her name. Kitchi's bravery matches his name. He is a great hunter of deer and bear as well as raccoon, beaver, and squirrel. Thus, Kitchi's family is always well feed despite his custom of sharing with families who are not so fortunate.

"What shall we name our son?" Nadie asks Kitchi.

"One day when I'm hunting, I see a white shining light coming from a glen. As I approach, a voice thunders out, warning me not to come closer, but to heed what is said. I fall down and hide my head in terror. I can barely utter the words. "Who are you, and what do you want of me?"

"I am Kisemanito; listen carefully to my words. You will soon have a son. You will name him Mingan because his life will be bound up with a gray wolf. He will become very wise in the ways of the forest spirits, and I have bestowed on him a gift I have not given to anyone else – the ability to converse with all the forest spirits and animals. He will become a great Shaman for your people." The great light then vanished.

Thus, Kitchi takes the baby in his arms and kisses him. "You will always be known as Mingan," he declares. Mingan spends all his time inside his parents' wigwam until his *walking out ceremony* as is the Cree custom, which dictates that a child's feet must never touch the ground until this ceremony. When the big day arrives, Nadie dresses Mingan in ceremonial deerskin, leggings and a fringed tunic. The whole family then sits at the entrance of their wigwam waiting for the elders. When they arrive and enter the wigwam, they tell Mingan to walk in a circle around the outside of the wigwam, and they show him how to mimic hunting deer and bear.

They then help Mingan complete this task. After Mingan reenters the wigwam, he gives the elders gifts of bear hides and beaver pelts that Kitchi provides. Afterwards there is a great feast; Mingan is the center of the festivities and enjoys all the attention he is receiving. The feasting and rejoicing continue late into the night, long after Mingan falls asleep in Nadie's arms.

As Mingan grows in stature, Kitchi teaches him all the ways of the hunt. Mingan becomes second only to Kitchi in his mastery of the bow and stalking games. As Mingan becomes older, his mischievous side also increases. He loves to play tricks on his older sister, Numees, such as tripping her when she carries water back to their wigwam. Numees then gets up and chases him with a stick and whips him as he tries to get away. He goes crying to Nadie who says, "Well, if you don't tease your sister, you won't have swats on your seat." Mingan has to agree in a begrudging manner. Thus, Mingan learns wisdom from Nadie, sometimes in an easy manner by just listening to her and sometimes the hard and painful way by experience. But in any case, Mingan gains knowledge that he will need in his future adventures.

One day, Kitchi comes into the wigwam and starts throwing everything around searching for something.

"What are you doing?" demands Nadie. "Why are you making such a mess?"

"I can't find my favorite bow. Did you take it?"

"No. Don't blame me. *You* are the one that's sloppy. Where did you last see it?"

"I don't know. It should be just outside our wigwam, but it's not there."

After both Kitchi and Nadie search every inch of the wigwam and scour the area outside, Nadie expresses a terrible fear she has. "I think that the forest spirit Apiscinis took it. Remember we didn't lay out our usual gifts of food for him last winter."

"Yes, but food was scarce during the winter, and we didn't have any to spare," replies Kitchi.

"I know," says Nadie, "But Apiscinis doesn't care. He's angry and will seek revenge on us. I fear taking your bow may only be the beginning. He may also seek to steal... (Nadie hesitates with a terrified look on her face). No! Mingan, listen very carefully. If you see a strong looking, hairy dwarf, run! Run for your life. That's how Apiscinis appears when he takes human form."

"We must keep Mingan close to our wigwam. Don't let him roam too far until we can appease Apiscinis," Kitchi declares as he hugs Mingan.

Nadie prepares some of Apiscinis's favorite treats and lays them out, but she still orders Mingan not to wonder off by himself because, once angered, Apiscinis is not easily placated. All goes well until Mingan's mischievous, impish nature wins its struggle with better sense.

Mingan taunts Numees by yelling, "Numees is sweet on Huritt. Numees loves Huritt."

Numees then picks up a switch and threatens, "You better stop saying that, or I'll swat you!"

"No you won't. You can't catch me," replies Mingan as he starts to run as fast as he can. Despite Nadie's warning, Mingan races out of their village with Numees in close pursuit. As they go deeper into the forest, Mingan hides in some deep brush and giggles to himself as he watches Numees rush by. He stays hidden for quite a while just to be sure that Numees won't see him. What Mingan doesn't know is that another pair of eyes does see him.

When Mingan emerges from the brush, he feels a bag being pulled over his head. No matter how much he thrashes about, he can't free himself. He then feels himself being lifted by someone and carried away. When Mingan continues to struggle, the bag is banged against a tree, and all goes black for Mingan.

When Mingan regains consciousness, everything is dark and blurry. Finally, his surroundings come into focus. He is in a small, windowless wigwam with a tiny hole in the ceiling, which is out of reach. The walls are formed by birch bark. It is lit by a fire in the middle of the room. Even though some of the smoke exits via the hole, most of the room is dense with the choking smoke. A huge clay pot hangs over the flames. In one corner are plates and cups carved out of wood. Mingan recognizes them as gifts his parents gave Apiscinis several winters ago. In another corner, he spies Kitchi's bow that Apiscinis has stolen, standing next to a large pouch that smells of fermented berries. The only entrance to the room is barred by a door made of log planks. The walls and door glow with a red color. Mingan tries to bash the door open, but it does not budge. He tries to smash through the walls, but again without success Finally, he gives up and crouches in a corner facing the door and waits.

After what seems like an eternity, the red color of the door fades, and it creaks open. A hairy dwarf with bulging muscles makes his way into the room lugging a deer hide full of water, some of which sloshes out as he plops it down. Mingan sees that the gnome is about his height, but is as wide as he is tall. He's dressed in tattered buckskin and has dirty, tangled hair. He glares at Mingan as he squats down on a mat. "It's all your parents' fault, you know. If only they had given me my tribute, you wouldn't be in this fix."

"But Mama put out food and other gifts for you. I saw her," pleads Mingan.

"Humph, not enough and too late. I don't need the food now when it's plentiful. I almost starved this winter. That's when I needed the food, and as for the gifts, they hardly make up for the suffering I have endured."

"You better let me go, or father will track you down and kill you," shouts Mingan with a defiant tone in his voice as he shakes his fist at Apiscinis.

"Just let him try," replies Apiscinis as he smashes his war club down on the ground and makes dirt fly up. "In any case you'll be my slave, cook my meals, clean this room, and fetch me my drink. Start by fixing these," and Apiscinis throws two dead hares on the ground next to Mingan. "Don't just sit there with your mouth open, get to work, or I'll bash you like I did these rabbits."

Mingan gets up and skins and cooks the hares as he has seen Nadie do many times. After Apiscinis gets his food, he yells for his drink. Mingan pours it out and gives it to Apiscinis who gulps it down in one go. He then yells for more.

After Apiscinis finishes his meal he shouts, "Clean up these dishes and the room. See that it's done before I return," and Apiscinis stomps out of the room and slams the door.

Mingan runs to the door and tries to open it, but it glows red and is locked. As Mingan looks at the dirty dishes, his impulse is to just throw the plates and cup into the fire, but then he remembers one of Nadie's stories.

There once were two braves. One is a foolish and impulsive brave, and the other is wise and patient. They both come to a raging river that is fed by snow melting in the mountains. The headstrong brave waits a short while, but finally gives into his emotions and announces, "You can stay if you want, but I am going to swim across now." Though he is a good swimmer, the current is too strong, and he drowns. The wise and patient brave waits many days. Finally, the snow all melts, and the river became calm. The patient brave then wades across the stream in safety. Nadie explains that the lesson of this story is to not let your emotions lead to your ruin, but be patient and wait for the proper moment to act. Then you will be delivered safely.

Mingan thus decides to bide his time. He washes Apiscinis's plate and cup and gathers up the bones from Apiscinis's meal. After gnawing off the meager amount of meat remaining on them, he throws the bones on the garbage pile in a corner of the wigwam, lies down on the dirt floor and goes to sleep. This pattern continues for many days, until one day Apiscinis comes in with terrible, bleeding gashes across his face.

"What happened?" Mingan exclaims with a horrified look.

"That damn bear monster, Kacitowaskw, slashed me with his giant paw for no reason at all except his evilness. Get me some drink to take away the pain."

As Mingan goes to get Apiscinis's cup, he spots a heavy log by the fireplace. He thinks, *Perhaps I can smash in Apiscinis's skull while he is in this weakened state and escape.* He is just about to pick up the log when another one of Nadie's stores rings in his head.

Once a brave is by a stream spearing fish. After he has caught enough for his family, he starts back to his village when he hears a crash behind him. When he turns around he sees a huge bear charging toward him. He quickly climbs a tree, but the bear starts to climb after him. The brave then throws the fish he caught to the ground, and the bear climbs down and makes off with the fish. Many days later the brave is again out in the forest, and he hears a fearful moaning. When he goes to investigate, he sees the same bear in agony with a huge thorn through his paw. At first the brave smiles and thinks that the bear is only getting what he deserves. But then the bear's cries of pain touch his heart, and he goes to the bear and pulls out the thorn and puts a healing salve on the wound. The bear then salutes him with his paw and lumbers off. Years later the brave finds himself surrounded by wolves who are about to tear him to bits. Suddenly, a bear crashes through the brush and drives off the wolves. He then goes to the brave and gives him a salute with his paw before sauntering off. It is the same bear he helped before! In time, after Nadie tells him this story, Mingan comes to understand that the point of this adage is to always listen to your heart and show kindness to others, even your enemies, and you will be rewarded. You may even turn an enemy into a friend.

So Mingan goes and gets Apiscinis's drink for him. He then starts to put a healing ointment from his pouch on Apiscinis's wounds.

Apiscinis yells out, "What are you doing there?"

"I'm just dressing your wound," Mingan replies as he continues to care for Apiscinis's injuries.

"Well, alright then, but get me some more drink," Apiscinis demands.

After many cups of his fermented juice, Apiscinis falls asleep and snores loudly. Mingan sees that the door has no red glow. He wonders, *Did Apiscinis forget to apply the spell to the door that prevents me from escaping?* He tries the door and finds he can open it. It creaks, but Apiscinis does not wake up. He grabs his father's bow and rushes out of the room into the fresh air of the forest. At last he is free! His mother was right! Once free, Mingan speeds away as fast as he can until he can run no more. As he bends over panting, he senses that he is being watched. As he starts to run again after catching his breath, he hears a voice,

"Don't fear. I want to help you."

Mingan looks around and is surprised to see a fox with a scarf on its head, standing on its hind legs. He quizzes, "Who are you?"

"I'm Grandmother Fox. I have adopted you and have advice and gifts to help you."

"Okay, but we must run, so Apiscinis doesn't catch us."

"You don't have to worry. Apiscinis isn't chasing you."

"How do you know?"

"There is little that goes on in the forest that I don't know. In fact, Apiscinis is no longer after you at all."

"But I escaped from him while he was asleep. He will surely be after me when he wakes up."

"How do you know he was asleep?"

"He drank so much fermented wine. He must have been asleep."

"I have never known Apiscinis not to be able to hold his drink."

Mingan then begins to wonder, *Could the moral of Mama's fable be true. Did my act of kindness change one as despicable as Apiscinis from an enemy to a friend?*

Mingan's thoughts are interrupted by Grandmother Fox's stern lecture. As she instructs, she wags her finger up and down to emphasize each point.

"Now listen carefully. You must watch for and avoid the evil spirits that lurk in the forest. Witiko is an evil spirit that's created from a brave that is guilty of selfishness, gluttony, or cannibalism. His evil so possesses his soul that he becomes a man-eating monster. When you cross a lake, beware of the Great Lynx spirit. In its physical form, it resembles a cross between a cougar and a dragon. It lives in deep water and can drag people down to the depths and drown them. But the most dangerous is Misikinebik, an underwater horned serpent that lurks in lakes and loves to dine on his favorite food, humans."

"How awful. Are there any others?" asks Mingan in a hesitant manner while he shakes in fear.

"Well there is Kacitowaskw, the stiff-jointed, hairless bear who has a savage look in his eyes and is blood thirsty."

"How can I survive against such monsters?" Mingan sobs in despair.

"That's why I'm here to help you my child," reassures Grandmother Fox, as she puts a paw on Mingan's shoulder. "I have many gifts here in this bag that will aid you in your journey back to your village. First of all, I have a bag of magic seeds and a bowl for you. If you are hungry or thirsty, just place a seed in the bowl and think of what kind of food or drink you want. It will appear." Grandmother Fox then digs deeper into her bag and declares, "Here is a magic stick. Suspend it, and it will show you the way to your village. I also have a canoe that will transport you across lakes and streams."

"But this canoe is no bigger than my hand. How can it carry me?" inquires Mingan.

"Just float it on water, and it will grow into a full-size canoe complete with paddles," replies Grandmother Fox, but remember, when you go on the water beware of the Great Lynx, but especially Misikinebik. To help protect you during your journeys across lakes, here is a clapper. When you wave it up and down, it will make a sound that will attract Piyesiws, the Thunder Birds. They make a sound like the crack of thunder when they beat their huge, powerful wings."

"Why would I want to summon such creatures?" asks Mingan with a puzzled look on his face.

"A fair question." replies Grandmother Fox. "The Piyesiw hate the Misikinebiķ and will drive them away. Another gift I have for you is a bee arrow."

"What is that, Grandmother Fox?" puzzles Mingan, "I've never heard of such a thing."

"Well, if you shoot this arrow and hit something, a swarm of bees will attack whatever is struck by the arrow. But use this arrow wisely, because it is the only one I have for you. Finally, here is some tobacco."

"But Grandmother Fox, my parents say I'm too young to smoke."

"Of course," Grandma Fox chuckles, "But this tobacco is not for you. It is for the Memekwesiw, the small, water dwelling spirits. They are a little smaller than you are. You can recognize them because they have no noses. They are not malicious, but like to play tricks on people who pass by. If you ignore them and give them no gifts, they may tip over your canoe; however, if you give them presents, particularly tobacco, they will befriend you. They even can be quite helpful."

Grandmother Fox then gives Mingan her final words of wisdom. "While these gifts will help you in your quest, it is your own wisdom in how you use them that will bring you safely home. Also, no matter how powerful these gifts are, your most effective weapon against all these evil forces are the friends you make along the way through acts of thoughtfulness. Remember that acts to kindness will always be rewarded." With those final words, Grandmother Fox disappears into a thicket.

Mingan gathers up all of Grandmother Fox's gifts except for the magic stick and puts them into his pouch. Then he carefully suspends the magic stick with a twine made out of braided vines and sets out in the direction it indicates. After Mingan walks for quite a while, he hears a frightful growling and a howling cry of agony. He runs toward the noise until he comes to a clearing. There he spots a giant hairless bear attacking a gray wolf who is trying to protect her pup. With one swipe of the bear's immense, dagger-tipped claw, he sends the wolf flying into a tree. There the wolf lies motionless with blood seeping from her wounds. The bear then turns toward the pup, who is cowering up against a tree. The bear raises his blood-stained claw, ready to dispatch the helpless pup. Mingan thinks, *This must be the Stiff-Jointed Bear, Kacitowaskw, that Grandmother Fox and Apiscinis told me about. How can I help this poor pup? My bee arrow; but should I use it? What if I need it later?* After looking at the hapless pup, Mingan makes his decision. He places the bee arrow's notch into the cord of his father's bow, pulls back, aims and fires. When the arrow strikes Kacitowaskw, he turns in a rage. Hatred glares from his yellow eyes. Just as he starts for Mingan, a huge swarm of bees descends on Kacitowaskw. He howls in furry as he swats at the air. He finally roars off into the forest with the bees in relentless pursuit.

Mingan runs over to the she-wolf. She is dead; she gave her life for her pup. Mingan then goes to the pup who is huddled in a ball shaking. When Mingan goes to pick up the pup, it emits a timid growl. This poor soul then cries a howl of mourning as it runs to the she-wolf and nuzzles her. After a while, Mingan pulls out his bowl, puts a seed in it, and thinks of wolf milk. The white liquid appears. He dips his finger and offers it to the pup to suck on. At first the pup refuses, but finally Mingan gains the pup's trust, and he sucks milk from Mingan's finger. Mingan then picks up the pup and sees it is a boy. "My name is Mingan, what's yours?"

The wolf cub replies in a meek voice, "Gray Wolf."

"That's what my name means," declares Mingan. "We are meant to be together." So Mingan cradles Gray Wolf in his arms and continues on his journey until night descends. Mingan and Gray Wolf settle in a glen for the night. While Mingan uses the magic seeds to fix them something to eat, Gray Wolf bites off and drags some branches from surrounding bushes over to make a bed. As they settle in for the night, darkness descends. In the middle of the night, Mingan and Gray Wolf awaken to the sound of growling and see eyes glaring in the darkness. As the threat closes in on them, Gray Wolf suddenly cries out. "No, don't hurt us, I am part of your pack, and this brave saved me from Kacitowaskw." The growls stop, and a wolf pack comes out of the shadows and into the moon light. "Gray Wolf, we were worried about you. Where is your mother?"

Gray Wolf lowers his head and cries as he blurts out, "Mama is dead. Kacitowaskw killed her."

The pack leader looks stunned and then howls in grief. He is soon joined by the rest of the pack. After the pack leader recovers, he says, "Gray Wolf, you should come with us. We will take care of you."

"No! Mingan saved me, and I can't desert him. He needs me."

"I'm touched by your loyalty, but you should go with your pack. They are your family," says Mingan.

"No, you are now my family," Gray Wolf insisted adamantly and takes his place beside Mingan. Thus, Mingan and Gray Wolf form a partnership that will last for their lifetime and beyond.

The wolf pack leader replies with a reluctant tone, "Okay, I see you are determined and are in good hands, but if you ever need our help, just howl."

The next night Mingan and Gray Wolf camp next to a fast running river. After they eat, they lie back on their bed of branches. A full moon gleams in the night sky illuminating their camp. As they stare at the moon, the *Man in the Moon* shines bright and then appears to come closer and closer. As Mingan and Gray wolf stare with their mouths wide open, the *Man in the Moon* falls onto the ground in front of them. Stumbling to his feet he apologizes, "I'm sorry. I hope you weren't startled."

"Who are you?" asks Mingan.

"I am Chahkabesh. You may know me as the *Man in the Moon*. Who are you?"

"I'm Mingan and this is Gray Wolf. How did you fall from the moon?"

"It's all quite embarrassing. I thought it might be fun to see how far in space I could jump. I leapt higher and higher until I landed here. Do you know how I can get back up to my place in the moon? I'm afraid that everyone will be disappointed when they don't see me up in my normal position."

"I don't know, but I think my mother, Nadie, may know. She is the wisest person in our tribe. We're on our way home, and you're welcome to join us."

"Oh, thank you. I will try not to be too much trouble." With that, Chahkabesh lies down next to Mingan and Gray Wolf and falls asleep. His loud snoring makes Mingan wonder if he did the right thing in inviting Chahkabesh to join them.

The next morning, after breakfast, they get ready to leave. When everything is packed, Chahkabesh looks around and asks, "How are we going to ride the river? Do you have a canoe?"

With that Mingan pulls the model canoe out of his bag.

Chahkabesh laughs, as he points at the little canoe. "You're kidding. Okay, the jokes over, where is your real canoe?"

"This is it," replies Mingan.

Then Chahkabesh begins to cry, "Why did I ever agree to go with these crazy people?"

But Mingan says, "Just watch." He carefully places the tiny canoe into the water while taking care to hang onto one end so it doesn't float away. As Chahkabesh and Gray Wolf watch in amazement, the canoe begins to grow in size until it is big enough to hold all of them. Chahkabesh stands dumbstruck with his mouth wide open.

"Ahh, how," he finally manages to babble.

"Here, hold this canoe while I load it," Mingan gestures to Chahkabesh. "Well, don't just stand there, get busy!"

"Oh sorry," utters Chahkabesh, and he *galoops* over in his clumsy manner to the canoe. Just as Mingan starts to throw Kitchi's bow into the canoe, a splash of water hits Mingan and Chahkabesh, followed by a giggling sound. This surprise foils Mingan's aim, and Kitchi's bow lands in the water. Chahkabesh immediately lets go of the canoe, picks up a stone and throws it at the heart of the splash. There is a brief cry, and then the splashing stops.

"No," yells Mingan. "Those must be the Memekwesiw, the water spirits. They don't mean any harm. Now look; you've let the canoe float away." They all watch as the canoe, carried by the current, disappears around the bend.

Chahkabesh bangs his head on the ground and moans, "Why am I so foolish? I always cause so much trouble."

The sign of his remorse quells Mingan's anger, and he pats Chahkabesh on the shoulder. Just then Gray wolf comes up to Mingan and drops the tobacco pouch at his feet. "Of course, if we give the Memekwesiw some tobacco, perhaps they will help us. Oh Gray Wolf, you are so smart," and Mingan cuddles him. Mingan then waits for the next time there is a splash in the river and throws the tobacco pouch at the center of the ripples in the water. A tiny hand emerges from the water, and the pouch disappears. They all sit down and wait, but nothing happens. As night approaches, they have their evening meal and lie down on a bed of leaves and bushes. They are awakened by a crashing sound and a terrible roar. By the moonlight showing from Chahkabesh's face, they see a monster with a huge protruding belly and a face that's distorted with hate. As he stomps toward Mingan and his band, they all shake with fear. Mingan grabs Gray Wolf and holds him to his breast. Suddenly a noseless, child-size figure appears out of the darkness, clutching a pipe in his mouth, which he removes. He then uses it to accentuate the gestures of his hand as he addresses the beast with no sign of fear.

"Witiko, you must leave my friends alone. Go back to the filth in which your selfishness and gluttony has condemned you."

"Memekwesiw, you water scum. How dare you address me in such a manner? I will devour both you and your friends."

"No you won't," fires back the Memekwesiw as he pulls out his knife.

Witiko then roars with laughter, "I'll grab you and bite off your head before you ever get close enough to use that puny blade."

The Memekwesiw says nothing but only gives a sly smile and puts his pipe back in his mouth. He pulls on the tip of the knife, and it stretches out to form an arrow. Then, from the darkness, he grabs Kitchi's bow that he had earlier retrieved from where it had fallen in the water. He threads the arrow and shoots the Witiko in the heart. The Witiko staggers for a bit and then falls to the ground dead. Next the Memekwesiw hands the bow to Mingan and, with a puff of smoke from his pipe, disappears into the shadows, leaving Mingan and his band gaping in amazement. None of them get any sleep that night, fearing the appearance of more Witikos, but no more challenge them. In the morning Mingan and the others all sit around a fire thankful for their deliverance from the Witiko, but ruing the loss of their canoe. They all jump when they hear a noise in the bushes. "Oh, it's only you Grandmother Fox," exclaims Mingan.

"Why, who were you expecting?"

"We thought it might be another Witiko," answers Mingan.

"Oh no. They won't dare bother you again. Didn't I tell you that friends you make will be more valuable than all the magic I can give you?"

"Yes, of course you're right, but now, we've lost our canoe. Can you help us again?"

"Just remember the lesson you learned in your interaction with Apiscinis, and you will be fine." With those words, Grandmother Fox disappears into a thicket.

"No! Wait! What did I learn?" Mingan pleads, but Grandmother Fox is gone. Mingan sits down on a log with his hands over his head in despair. Gray Wolf comes up to him and pulls on his pants leg and says, "Don't be dismayed! Just think about what you learned. I know you can do it."

"You're right Gray Wolf. I must remember what my experience taught me." Finally, Mingan declares, "I have it. I assumed that

Apiscinis was asleep when he was not. He let me go on purpose because of my kindness. So I learned I should not just assume things. I have believed the canoe is lost, when it may not be!" With that Mingan races along the shore of the riverbank and, sure enough, around a bend in the river the canoe has been caught in the branches of a tree that had fallen into the river. Mingan yells, "Thank you! Thank you! Grandmother Fox."

In reply, a faint voice comes from deep in the forest, "Also beware of too much of a good thing."

Mingan looks around, but sees no one. He yells, "How can I have too much of a good thing?" But all he hears in return are his friends crashing through the bushes towards him. Mingan's mind returns to the situation at hand and yells for them to bring all their gear while he pulls the canoe to the shore. Once the canoe is packed, they head out again with Mingan paddling in the rear and Chahkabesh in front. At first Chahkabesh is more of a hindrance than a help, splashing everyone while trying to paddle. Gray Wolf shakes the water from his coat while Mingan yells, "Chahkabesh stop! Just watch me." Chahkabesh turns around and watches Mingan as he paddles with long smooth strokes. After many attempts and teaching sessions by Mingan, Chahkabesh finally catches on enough so that they can make progress. They are aided by the fact that they are going with the current rather than against it. The gentle breeze is soothing as they glide along through the fresh smelling forest. *How peaceful and beautiful it is*, Mingan thinks. *It is such a good thing that we are floating with the current. Wait a minute. The voice said to beware of too much of a good thing. Can it be?* Just then Mingan hears a faint roar and sees a cloud of mist rising in the distance. He also feels the current become stronger.

"Waterfall ahead!" screams Mingan with terror in his voice. "Paddle for the shore, for your lives! No Chahkabesh, paddle on the same side as me!" Mingan screams in desperation.

Despite all their efforts, Mingan has spotted the falls too late. The current is dragging them towards their doom. Just as the lip of the falls comes into view, a tree crashes down in front of them, blocking their descent to the rocks below.

"Grab the tree trunk Chahkabesh!" yells Mingan.

Chahkabesh wraps his arms around a huge branch and holds on with all his strength. Mingan crawls to the front of the canoe and together they manage to drag the canoe to the shore. Even Gray Wolf bites small tree branches and tries to help. When they reach the shore, they drag the canoe up on the sandy beach and then collapse with exhaustion. After they all recover, Mingan takes a careful look at the base of their savior tree. It has clearly been gnawed by beavers, but none are in sight, and Mingan didn't see any beaver dams on the river or its inlets. Mingan thinks, *I wonder if this is the doing of Grandmother Fox.*

Just then his thoughts are interrupted by Gray Wolf, "Shouldn't we be going? My fur is getting drenched from the mist of the waterfall."

"You're right," declares Mingan, and they ready themselves to portage around the falls. Chahkabesh asks, "Why isn't the canoe shrinking in size now that it is out of the water?"

"I don't know," replies Mingan. "Maybe the mist from the falls is keeping it wet."

"Let's wait and see if it gets smaller. I'm don't want to have to lift it," laments Chahkabesh. "I'm too clumsy to carry things."

"Let's have lunch first and see what happens," replies Mingan as he pulls out the magic seeds and bowl. So they all eat and keep a watchful eye on the canoe.

"I think it may be getting a little smaller," says Chahkabesh in a hopeful voice.

"No, I don't think so. We will just have to carry it." With that Mingan slings the bag of their possessions over his shoulder and picks up the front of the canoe. "Come on Chahkabesh, pick up the other end," commands Mingan.

Chahkabesh groans, but obliges. The way around the falls is steep and muddy, thanks to the mist from the falls. The descent is made more difficult by Chahkabesh, who keeps tripping over bushes and roots. Every time he falls, he and Mingan tumble down the slope a ways and must struggle to their feet to continue. Finally, they manage to work their way around the falls and can drop their load on a downstream bank. Soaked and muddy, they look up at the beauty of their nemesis as it tumbles down and crashes onto the rocks below. A sense of dread grips Mingan as he contemplates what their fate might have been if the fallen tree had not intervened. The more he thinks of it, the more convinced he becomes that Grandmother Fox must have saved them once again.

After washing off the mud from themselves and drying in the sun, the band loads up the canoe again and continues their journey. However, they keep a wary eye out for the signs of another waterfall. Fortunately, they do not encounter anymore before they come to a large lake. The magic dangling stick indicates they must cross the lake, but it's already evening, and they decide to camp here for the night. They drag the canoe onto the shore and watch it shrink as it dries. After a quick meal, they go to sleep on some leaves and shrubs they have formed into a bed.

They wake up in the morning to a strong wind and threatening storm clouds overhead.

"We must hurry and cross the lake before the waves are too high," Mingan warns.

They gather all their belonging and are just about to put the canoe in the water, so it can grow to full size, when they hear a squeaking call for help.

Chahkabesh yells, "Never mind. We must go immediately!"

However, Mingan pays no heed and investigates the cry. As he spreads the shrubs aside, he sees a skunk caught in a trap. Holding his nose, Mingan moves to free the animal. In response, the skunk raises its tail ready to spray.

"No! Please! I only want to help," yells Mingan as he ducks.

The skunk hesitates and then lowers its tail. Mingan quickly frees the skunk from the snare obtaining a sulfur smell on his hands for his efforts.

"Thank you. You saved my life. I'm sorry about the smell. Tell me how I can help you."

"That's okay, I really must go now." With that Mingan runs to the others. They put the canoe in the water. After it has a chance to grow to full size, they load it and set off. As they paddle along, the wind becomes ever stronger, and the waves start to splash over the side of the canoe. Then in the distance, Mingan spots a giant wave headed right for them. Cougar eyes of the Great Lynx glare at them from its crest and a green scaly dragon's body forms its base. "Paddle for your life, away from that wave!" screams Mingan above the roar of the storm. Gray Wolf barks his encouragement, and Mingan buries his paddle hand into the waves straining with all his strength, but no matter how hard he and Chahkabesh paddle, the wave keeps coming closer and closer. The Great Lynx glares from the torrent and chortles with glee as he declares,

"I will drown you who dared to brave my waters. Prepare to meet your doom."

Just as the wave is about to engulf them, a giant fish leaps from the deep and swallows the wave, saving Mingan and his band. Mingan and his crew manage to struggle the canoe to the shore where they collapse in relief. Just as they gain their breath, the giant fish beaches itself on the shore. Mingan, Chahkabesh, and Gray Wolf leap backwards in fear. But then the fish starts to shrink, its fins develop fingers and its tail grows feet. Finally, when the metamorphosis is complete, a powerful warrior stands before them.

"Don't be afraid, I only want to help you."

"But who are you, and how did you manage..."

"I am Ayas, and I have the power to change from my human form to become any animal I choose. You saved me, so saving you was the least I could do."

"But when did I save you," asked Mingan.

"Remember when you saved the skunk? That was me. I was trapped in a magic snare that a Witiko set for me. I could only be saved by someone who cared for me, a skunk, more than their own safety. I would not have been able to change form and save you if you hadn't helped me first."

Ayas's words made Mingan recall Grandmother Fox's sage advice, *Remember that acts of kindness will always be rewarded.*

"Won't you stay and eat with us?" Mingan asks Ayas.

"Well, I guess I have some free time, and, because I was trapped, I haven't eaten for days. Besides the Great Lynx left a terrible taste in my mouth that some good food and drink might dispel." So Ayas sits down on a log, which groans under his weight.

Mingan takes out his magic seeds and bowl and asks. "What would you like first?"

"Fermented berry juice to sweeten all the Great Lynx's foul residue in my mouth." So Mingan prepares and hands Ayas bowl after bowl of the drink, which he always slurps up with a single gulp. Finally, Ayas indicates he is ready for some food. Again, Mingan hands Ayas many bowls of deer, moose and bear meat. For dessert, Ayas requests bowls of sweet, fresh berries. Finally, after many hours Ayas announces,

"Ahh, that is a great snack, but I must now go and help others that I sense are in danger." With that, Ayas lifts his mighty frame and strides off into the woods, leaving Mingan with mixed feelings.

While Mingan enjoys Ayas's company and the feeling of security he provides, Mingan is concerned about how many magic seeds he had to use to provide Ayas his *snack*. He shudders to think how many seeds he would need for one of Ayas's proper meals! All the day's excitement leaves Mingan and his band quite exhausted, so they decide to camp on the edge of the lake overnight.

They wake up to the call of the loons and a morning mist over the lake. When Mingan goes to the lake to fetch some water, he sees a mother loon with her baby on her back paddling towards him. She is quickly joined by a multitude of other loons.

One of the loons and his mate exclaim, "Thank you. We are oh so grateful that you freed this lake of the Great Lynx. He was always threatening us and our babies. If there is ever anything we can do, just let us know, and we will be happy to aid you."

"That is kind of you, but it was actually Ayas who destroyed the Great Lynx," says Mingan bowing his head in modesty.

"Well whoever did it has earned our eternal gratitude, but I'm sure you are being too modest. Our offer of friendship still stands," states the male loon as he floats away.

When Mingan returns with the water, he and his crew prepare breakfast, pack their belongings and set out through the forest. The farther into the forest they go, the fewer bird songs they hear, and the denser and darker the forest becomes. If it was not for the magic dangling stick, they would have never made it out of the tangle of trees and brush. As they go deeper and deeper into the forest, the sunlight becomes completely blocked by the surrounding canopy of the forest. Mingan and Chahkabesh must endure the scratches of the branches as they push them aside, and Gray Wolf becomes covered with brambles. All of a sudden, they hear a crashing of the greenery. The heavy trod of footsteps crunches the long-fallen leaves. Two bloodshot, yellow eyes glare at Mingan and his band.

A voice thunders forth, "I am Kacitowaskw. The last time we met, you set a multitude of bees on me. I still have welts from their stings. At the time, I swore you would feel the same pain and worse, and I have tracked you throughout all your travels. I saw the Great Lynx attack you and hoped he would fail, so I can have the pleasure of seeing you suffer as I slash you to death. Now I will have my revenge."

As Kacitowaskw starts to advance with his giant dagger-tipped claws raised, Mingan and Chahkabesh cower in fear. Just as Kacitowaskw is ready to strike, Gray Wolf rushes forward and bites the monster; he then runs between Kacitowaskw's legs before he can react. As Gray Wolf returns to Mingan's side, he starts to howl. Kacitowaskw staggers back in surprise, but soon gathers himself. Mingan suddenly realizes what Gray Wolf is doing and yells to Chahkabesh,

"Join in Gray Wolf's call and howl as loud as you can."

Chahkabesh doesn't understand why, but decides this is no time to question Mingan's commands, and he adds his voice.

"Do you really think all your infernal noise will save you?" sneers Kacitowaskw.

Just then there are answering howls that seem to come from all directions, and suddenly hundreds of eyes begin to appear in the darkness. The growling is deafening. Then there is a deluge of teeth and claws against slashing paws. The melee ends with Kacitowaskw howling in retreat pursued by packs of wolves with Kacitowaskw's blood and skin in their teeth. Mingan grabs Gray Wolf and cuddles him.

"Gray Wolf, you have saved us again. What would I do without you? I love you forever."

When the wolves reassembled after chasing Kacitowaskw deep into the forest, the leader addresses Gray Wolf.

"You indeed have shown your bravery and resourcefulness. We again ask you to join our pack."

Gray Wolf answers with humility, "I am deeply honoured by your invitation, but my friends here are my family. Besides, I have to stick with them to keep them out of trouble."

The pack leader nods in agreement and, together with the others, disappears into the forest. Mingan and his friends struggle all day through the brush until they emerge at another lake. They collapse in exhaustion on the bank and fall asleep without even eating or preparing a bed. When they wake up, Mingan uses his magic bowl to feed everyone and then prepares a salve to relieve the itching and pain from the scratches he and Chahkabesh incurred. He then sits down with Gray Wolf and removes the brambles from his coat in as careful and gentle a manner as he can. Once they have recovered from their ordeal of travelling through the dense forest, they all help pack the canoe and set out across the lake. There is no wind, so the lake is smooth and glassy with only gentle ripples from the gliding of the canoe. The surface shines with the warmth of the sunlight and mirrors the blue of the cloudless sky. The far shore reflects the green trees and shrubs on its bank. Mingan also spots deer bringing their fawns down to the water to drink. Ducks paddle by, quacking as the canoe glides along. This idyllic scene causes everyone in the canoe to relax so much they become drowsy.

Suddenly the ducks begin to make a racket and flap their wings in a furious manner, before all take flight away from the lake. When Mingan looks to the shore, he sees that the deer and their fawns have disappeared. Then waves begin to appear in the lake.

"Row, row for shore, fast!" yells Mingan to Chahkabesh, waking him from his reverie, but it's too late.

The head of the horned serpent, Misikinebik, breaks through the water and hisses at them,

"How dare you trespass on my domain. Now you will pay with your lives. I'll suck you down into the depths of the lake and then devour you all."

With that, Misikinebik's long body starts to encircle the canoe, creating a vortex that turns into a whirlpool. Down, down into the maelstrom Mingan and his friends are sucked as the waves bang the canoe's occupants back and forth against the sides of the canoe. Gray Wolf just manages to grab the clapper out of their bag of possessions before it is swept over the side as Misikinebik's mighty tail slams against the side of their craft. As Gray Wolf is tumbled around inside the canoe, he manages to show the clapper to Mingan who grabs it and uses it to make a frantic, clapping sound. Just as the canoe is about to be swept under, thunder begins to echo throughout the forest, shaking the water like an earthquake. The swirling of the water abates as quickly as it began as Misikinebik's body becomes motionless. Then overhead the sky becomes black with an army of Piyesiws, the thunderbirds. The ground shakes from the powerful beating of their wings.

Misikinebik yells as he swims away and dives for his life, "Curse you for calling the Piyesiw."

Then suddenly the Piyesiw descend below the waves and their fearsome teeth and claws take chunks out of Misikinebik's flesh as he dives to the very depths of the lake and disappears. Only a few bubbles remain from his presence, and they quickly dissipate. Then a huge explosion of Piyesiw breaks through the surface of the water, and they disappear over the horizon as suddenly as they appeared. Mingan, Chahkabesh, and Gray Wolf are left awestruck. When they recover, Mingan and Chahkabesh use their hands to row to shore since their paddles where swept overboard during Misikinebik's attack.

Mingan takes Gray Wolf in his arms and caressing him says, "You saved us once again. What would have become of us without you?"

"Remember I said you needed me," replies Gray Wolf, who then proceeds to lick Mingan's hands and face.

Chahkabesh also praises Gray Wolf as he shines as bright on him as a full moon. However, once they recover from their ordeal, a harsh reality sets in.

Chahkabesh laments, "We have lost all our possessions. Without our magic seeds and bowl, how will we eat? Without the pointing stick, how will we know where to go? Perhaps we should have just drowned in the lake instead of wandering around until we starve to death."

Mingan has just opened his mouth ready to respond to Chahkabesh, when he hears a loon's cry. The loon couple they met before lands on the water and approaches them.

"Can we help you?" asks the male loon as he swims up to Mingan.

"All our possessions are at the bottom of the lake, and now we are going to starve to death," cries Chahkabesh.

"That's no problem. Loons are the very best lake divers," boasts the male loon with his chest puffed out. "Tell us where you lost them, and my mate and I will retrieve them."

Mingan points to the center of the lake. Both loons dive for a long time, but they find nothing.

"Thank you anyway," yells Mingan. "We'll just have to make do without them."

"Loons don't give up so soon," announce both loons at the same time.

With that the loon belt out their haunting refrain. Soon, a few dozen loons arrive who also take up the call. Finally, thousands of loons appear and all of them start diving into the lake. First, they recover the pointing stick. Then they find the sack with the magic seeds and the bowl. In addition, they retrieve Kinchi's bow, which was knocked overboard during Misikinebik's attack. They even located the oars, but they cannot grab ahold of them. Then Gray Wolf springs into action. He swims to the spot the loons indicate, dives down and one by one brings up the oars in his teeth and swims them to shore. He then showers Mingan and Chahkabesh, who are running to greet him, with water as he shakes his coat. They both roar with laughter.

"How can we ever thank you all?" asks Mingan as he gestures towards the loons who now completely blanket the water around Mingan and his band.

"No! It is we who must thank you for ridding us of the menace from The Great Lynx and Misikinebik. Now we and our chicks will be safe and can float peacefully on the water. Just remember when you hear our call, we will always be your friends."

After the loons fly off, Mingan and his band follow the pointing stick into the forest.

Several days later, Mingan yells, "I recognize this place. I know where we are!"

He starts to run and the others struggle to keep up. Finally, they all arrive back at Mingan's village. When Nadie sees him, she drops the basket she is making and, with tears streaming down her cheeks, runs and enfolds Mingan in her arms. When she finally releases her son, he is embraced by Kitchi. Mingan and his band are soon encircled by the whole village. Mingan is quick to introduce Chahkabesh and Gray Wolf to everyone.

"I would not have made it back to you without their help," Mingan announces.

Everyone then embraces Chahkabesh and Gray Wolf. Later, while Mingan, Chahkabesh, and Gray Wolf rest, Nadie and Kitchi organize a great celebration. When all is ready, the chief and the whole tribe welcome Mingan, Chahkabesh and Gray Wolf with a formal ceremony. After the welcoming speeches and dancing, everyone enjoys a huge feast. Finally, it is time for Mingan to relate his adventures. All are seated in a circle around Mingan, and he begins his tale. He starts by showing Kitchi's bow and telling how Apiscinis steals it because he feels wronged. He then says that despite warnings from his parents, his foolish behavior allows Apiscinis to kidnap him and causes Nadie and Kitchi such worry and pain. Mingan goes on to describe how remembering his mother's stories causes him to show kindness to Apiscinis that in turn results in his release. He then relates how the gifts of Grandmother Fox aid him in his attempt to return home. He presents and describes the small canoe and paddles to the Cree Chief. He further gives the chief the magic seeds and bowl and explains that they can provide food for the tribe in times of need. The members of the tribe roar when Mingan tells how Kacitowaskw was sent fleeing from the swarm of bees after he was hit by the bee arrow. Mingan goes on to describe how Witiko was defeated by one of the Memekwesiw, the great Lynx was conquered by Ayas, and Misikinebik beaten by the Piyesiw. Mingan then presents the clapper used to call the Piyesiw to the chief. Mingan also describes how they were aided by the loons and that the tribe should revere them from now on. Finally, Mingan declares that most of the credit for their return should go to his two companions, Chahkabesh and Gray Wolf, and he pats Chahkabesh on the back and cradles Gray Wolf in his arms. With those words Mingan sits down. Everyone in the tribe, especially Nadie and Kitchi, are greatly impressed by not only his bravery, but especially by his wisdom and modesty.

When the celebration is over, Nadie and Kitchi take Mingan and Gray Wolf back to their wigwam. Before they go inside, Mingan asks his parents to sit with him for a while before they go to sleep.

"I have a question that has been bothering me for a while. Why did Kisemanito let me be kidnapped by Apiscinis?"

Nadie thinks a moment and then says, "Before you were born, Kisemanito appeared to Kitchi in a vision and told him we are going to have a son who will be a great Shaman and advise our people with wisdom and insight using his ability to communicate with all the forest animals and spirits. Before you had your great adventure, do you think the mischievous and headstrong boy you were could have fulfilled this role?"

Mingan bows his head and replies, "No mother. I don't think so. I have learned so much on my travels that I would not have known otherwise. I can see now why my ordeal was necessary."

"Yes son, you have learned the lessons well that Kisemanito set for you, so you can fulfill your future role as Shaman."

With that, Kitchi and Nadie enter the wigwam. Before Mingan goes in with Gray Wolf, he hears Chahkabesh sighing in the distance while staring up at the faceless moon. Mingan then remembers his promise to Chahkabesh that he will help him get home and thinks, *I must consult my mother about Chahkabesh tomorrow. She will know what to do.*

The next day after talking to Nadie, Mingan goes out and finds Chahkabesh who has tears in his eyes.

"I'm sorry, I don't mean to put a damper on your festivities. It is wonderful that you and Gray Wolf are home now. I just wish..." Mingan interrupts him,

"It's all going to be okay. I've already talked with my mother. She is the wisest person I know, and she says there is a way to get you back to your home on the moon."

Chahkabesh smiles with his brightest moon-glow and hugs Mingan in joy. That night Nadie and the whole village accompany Chahkabesh out into a large meadow underneath the featureless, full moon. Nadie unfolds a huge spread that is made of many deerskins sewed together. They double the spread and then double it again, so it is very strong; yet it is still large enough that the whole village can grab ahold of it. After Chahkabesh embraces Mingan for a long time, he sobs

"I'm glad to go home, but I will miss you and Gray Wolf so much."

"But we will see each other every night; whenever Gray Wolf and I look up at the moon," replies Mingan as he embraces Chahkabesh for a last time.

Chahkabesh nods in agreement and hugs everyone else. He then walks to the center of the spread. The whole village grabs hold of a portion of the blanket and begins to toss Chahkabesh up into the air. The first toss throws him about ten meters high. Each successive toss throws him higher and higher. As they continue, he is now almost out of sight after they toss him. One final heave, and he no longer comes back. When they look up at the moon, they see Chahkabesh's happy, shinning face. The whole village cheers. Mingan and Gray Wolf continue to stare at their friend long after everyone else has gone. They feel such joy that their comrade is at last home and can beam down on them.

Mingan does grow up to be a great Shaman. He uses his courage and wisdom he gained from his journey to advise about the Forest Spirits and help the tribe out of their troubles. Gray Wolf is his constant, trusted companion who uses his great knowledge of the forest creatures to help Mingan. Their fame spreads well beyond their own village. At their death, Kisemanito is so pleased with their selfless service that he makes them great and powerful forest spirits. So, whenever faced with problems, the chief and elders go to the woods and give a wolf howl to summon Mingan and Gray Wolf. Gray Wolf then howls in return, and Mingan and Gray Wolf appear and give good council and protection against evil. Thus,

Mingan and Gray Wolf become the greatest and best of the Forest Spirits.

Mingan and Gray Wolf

Picture by Sylvia Sass (Used with permission)

Attawapiskat

(ᐋᐦᑕᐧᐋᐱᔅᑳᐧᐃ ᐃᓂᓂᐧᐊᐠ)

For centuries we live by the James Bay shore.
Our men fish and hunt with pride,
The geese and caribou nature does provide.
Our homes are wigwams built with a foundation of poles.
We then add bark, skins to keep out the cold.
In winter, earthen sod banishes snow from within,
And keeps us from freezing by taming the wind.
Our elders know when to move to escape,
Floods from the ice jams the Attawapiskat River does make.
So in Summer and Spring in Attawapiskat we live,
But in winter time, away we do roam,
Hunting and trapping sites far away are made home.
Everyone is busy, everyone has their tasks.
Everyone has their purpose, everyone self-respect.
We live in an Eden, in paradise here.
The mountains, spruce covered, the waters pristine.
We share them with brothers, the caribou and moose.
We share them with geese, ducks and muskrat,
With beaver, bear, wolves, and otters we trap.
Nature provides for all in her bounty and care.
In return we all love her with the greatest respect.
We are in the land and the land is in us.
The land is our heart, the land is our soul.
Who are we?
We are the Cree. *People of the parting rocks.*
We are proud. We are free. A noble tribe of humanity.

Shakespeare: I wrote this story and poem as a tribute to the native people for their love of the land and all its inhabitants. In their legends and stories they teach us how we should revere animals and give them the respect they so richly merit.

Acknowledgements

PHOTOGRAPHS FROM SHUTTERSTOCK are acknowledged where they are located in the text.

The photograph, *Buddy*, was photographed by Laura R. Morris and is used with permission.

The painting, *Mingan and Gray Wolf*, is by Sylvia Sass and is reproduced with permission.

All photographs except those acknowledged above are taken and copy written by Vincent L. Morris, © 2019.

Shakespeare and I want to thank Margaret Bird, Ann Morris, Winn Files, and Lyn Hill for proof reading this book and making very valuable suggestion. We also want to express our gratitude to the Grand Bend Writers' Group for their invaluable assistance and encouragement.

About the Authors

VINCENT L. MORRIS WAS BORN in Youngstown, Ohio and lived in the United States until 1976 when he, his wife Ann and his two daughters, Lynn and Laura, moved to Canada. He attended the University of California at Berkeley and graduated with a B.A. in Physics and Biology in 1964. He earned his Ph.D. in Biophysics at the University of Chicago in 1969, doing his research on herpes simplex virus in the laboratory of Dr. Bernard Roizman. He then served in the U.S. Air Force for four years. After his tour of duty, he completed post-doctoral studies on mouse mammary tumor virus with Drs. J. Michael Bishop and Harold Varmus in 1976. He then joined the Department of Microbiology and Immunology at the University of Western Ontario in London, Ontario, where he still resides with his wife and, of course, his comrade, Shakespeare. During his scientific career, Vincent has published more than seventy articles in scientific journals. After his retirement, Vincent took advantage of his experience in writing papers, reports and grant requests, to take up literary writing. He has written articles for the newspaper, *The Examiner*, published in Exeter, Ontario. He has also published a book of poetry entitled, *Love's Passion, Pleasure Through Poetry*. Two short stories, "My Unstoppable Great Aunt" and "My Algonquin Adventure" have been published in the literary magazine, *Canadian Stories*.

Shakespeare "collie" Morris was born in South Western Ontario. He currently resides with his friend and writing partner, Vince Morris. Shakespeare has revealed that "Shakespeare" is really his *nom de plume*, chosen since he is a shameless bardolater; however, he prefers to keep his real name a secret. Shakespeare has no formal education, but he reads voraciously. It seems that no school will award him the degrees in linguistics and English that he so obviously deserves. Not only does he merit a Ph.D. in foreign languages, but a University should hire him, as he would be the only faculty member that is fluid in Dog, Horse and Cat as well as English. I have no doubt that he could learn any other language with ease. Think of the research advances that would be possible if we could tap into the wisdom of all of these animals. Of course, his writing speaks for itself. Unfortunately, the narrow-minded Nobel Prize committee has barred dogs from receiving their awards. Shakespeare only hopes that the reading public will not be so prejudice against dogs as Universities and award committees obviously are!

Vince and Shakespeare

35805072R00125

Made in the USA
Lexington, KY
08 April 2019